PENGUIN

MAXIMS AN

JOHANN WOLFGANG VON GOETHE was born in Frankfurt am Main in 1749. He studied law in Leipzig and in Strasbourg, where Herder introduced him to Shakespeare and to folk song. Under his influence he produced some of the most famous poems in the German language, and at twenty-four wrote *Götz von Berlichingen*, a play which brought him national fame and established him at the forefront of the 'Storm and Stress' movement. *Werther*, a tragic novel of unfulfilled love, was an even greater success. Goethe began work on *Faust* and on *Egmont*, another tragedy, before being invited for a brief stay with an admirer, the Grand Duke of Weimar. It was in Weimar, however, that he was to spend most of his life, much of it in government service. Frustrations and an interest in the classical world led him to leave suddenly for Italy in 1786, and the two-year absence that followed saw the beginnings of the dramas *Iphigenie on Tauris* and *Torquato Tasso*, while *Italian Journey* recounts his wealth of experiences in the country. Back in Weimar, friendship with Schiller was to prove another source of inspiration, and a steady stream of publications was to flow until his death. The most notable of Goethe's later achievements were the two volumes of *Wilhem Meister* and the ambiguous *Elective Affinities*, and, in drama, the second part of *Faust*. Besides his writing Goethe directed the State Theatre and worked on numerous aspects of natural science. He married his long-standing mistress in 1806 and died in 1832, soon after completing *Faust*.

ELISABETH STOPP was born in 1911 and died in 1996, shortly after completing her translation of Goethe's maxims. She taught in Cambridge for many years, writing extensively on medieval French saints as well as numerous aspects of German literature. Her principal publications include *Madame de Chantal, Portrait of a Saint, German Romantics in Context* and a translation of letters by François de Sales.

PETER HUTCHINSON lectures in German at Cambridge, where he is Fellow and Librarian of Trinity Hall. He has worked widely as an editor of German texts and his publications include *Games Authors Play* and *Stefan Heym: The Perpetual Dissident*.

JOHANN WOLFGANG VON
GOETHE

Maxims and Reflections

Translated by ELISABETH STOPP

Edited with an Introduction and Notes by
PETER HUTCHINSON

PENGUIN BOOKS

In memory of Frederick J. Stopp MBE
the royalties from this volume will benefit
The Royal Star & Garter Home
for Disabled Sailors, Soldiers and Airmen.

PENGUIN BOOKS

Published by the Penguin Group
Penguin Books Ltd, 80 Strand, London WC2R 0RL, England
Penguin Putnam Inc., 375 Hudson Street, New York, New York 10014, USA
Penguin Books Australia Ltd, 250 Camberwell Road, Camberwell, Victoria 3124, Australia
Penguin Books Canada Ltd, 10 Alcorn Avenue, Toronto, Ontario, Canada M4V 3B2
Penguin Books India (P) Ltd, 11 Community Centre, Panchsheel Park, New Delhi – 110 017, India
Penguin Books (NZ) Ltd, Cnr Rosedale and Airborne Roads, Albany, Auckland, New Zealand
Penguin Books (South Africa) (Pty) Ltd, 24 Sturdee Avenue, Rosebank 2196, South Africa

Penguin Books Ltd, Registered Offices: 80 Strand, London WC2R 0RL, England

www.penguin.com

Published in Penguin Books 1998

030

Translation copyright © the Estate of Elisabeth Stopp, 1998
Introduction and Notes copyright © Peter Hutchinson, 1998

Set in 10/12.5 pt PostScript Monotype Bembo
Typeset by Rowland Phototypesetting Ltd, Bury St Edmunds, Suffolk
Printed and bound in Great Britain by Clays Ltd, Elcograf S.p.A.

www.greenpenguin.co.uk

Penguin Books is committed to a sustainable
future for our business, our readers and our planet.
This book is made from Forest Stewardship
Council™ certified paper.

Contents

Preface

The late Elisabeth Stopp was equally at home in the fields of literature, theology and translation. Her many articles on the German Romantics were rewarded with the Eichendorff Medal of the *Eichendorff-Gesellschaft*, the highest honour in this field, while her book on the French Jeanne de Chantal earned her a Fellowship of the Royal Society of Literature. She was at her strongest in combining literary and linguistic analysis, and translation – from German, French and Latin – was thus her forte. Her aim was not simply perfect sense, but tone and rhythm which would match the original.

Goethe was one of Elisabeth's favourite authors, and her fascination with his way of creating, together with her thorough knowledge of all aspects of his life and work, allowed her to translate confidently the entire collection of his maxims and reflections. She worked on these sporadically for over ten years, and had completed the translation and some of the notes shortly before her death on 4 November 1996. Although she had made a large collection of jottings on what others had written about the maxims, Elisabeth could not bring herself to shape these into an introduction. In retrospect the reason for this is clear: she saw the present work as her last great literary endeavour, and to complete it would have signalled the end of her scholarship. This was not something she could face with equanimity.

I promised Elisabeth that I would ensure the manuscript reached print, and I have therefore finalized the preparation for print, written the Introduction, Further Reading and Note on the Text to the present volume, and prepared the Notes. I have also made small changes to some of the translations. In all other respects the work is hers.

P.H.

Introduction

Johann Wolfgang von Goethe, Germany's greatest writer and one of the last of those great 'Universal Men' who had stalked Europe since the Renaissance, was born in Frankfurt am Main on 28 August 1749. His life was rich, hectic and long, and his contribution to science was, in his own eyes, almost as important as his achievements in literature. For Goethe was an anatomist and geologist as well as a composer of masterpieces in every literary genre. He was a botanist and a thinker as well as a critic and a translator. He was, in addition, a fine pictorial artist and theatre director as well as being an outstanding administrator and Privy Councillor. He has been claimed as the greatest German mind that has ever lived, and although much of his scientific writing was not taken seriously by his contemporaries or his successors, his literary shadow fell starkly over every writer to follow him. His death in 1832 ended what was to become known as the 'Age of Goethe'.

Goethe's maxims represent a small part of a massive output. They are remarkably varied not simply because they gestated over many years and because their author was so versatile, but also because Goethe was so receptive to cultures outside his own. He drew inspiration from an array of sources, and of particular importance for the patterns of thinking and composition which he adopts in the maxims, one would point especially to the Bible and to the Classics (the terse, balanced statements of Proverbs and Ecclesiastes in the Old Testament, the epigrams of Martial and of Linnaeus, the aphorisms of Hippocrates). He was also a reader of other writers of aphorisms and of those with a particularly concise style, such as Montaigne, Pascal and La Rochefoucauld, not to mention the greatest aphorist of the German language, his compatriot

Lichtenberg. Yet there were many other books and individuals who influenced his approach, including, at various stages, the Koran, Chinese poetry, Persian poetry and Laurence Sterne.

Born into a wealthy and prestigious family, Goethe enjoyed a strongly supportive background and a privileged education. He was precocious and self-confident, and his early compositions were in a variety of languages, including English. Aged sixteen he began to study law in Leipzig, and then, after an illness, in Strasbourg. It was here that he fell deeply in love, one of many emotional attachments throughout his life which were to inspire some of his greatest poetry, and where he met the thinker and critic Herder, who was to change his conception of German culture and encourage him to break firmly with the Germans' preference for French literary models. Study played only a relatively small part in Goethe's eventful life of this time, but part of his experience here would be exposure to the maxim form as a means of teaching both law and the sciences in the easily memorable mode of brief, pithy statements.

After completing his studies and obtaining his doctorate (having dabbled in various other subjects, including literature, drawing, chemistry and anatomy), Goethe returned to Frankfurt, where he was soon to write the two works for which he remained most famous throughout his life: *Götz von Berlichingen* (1771, revised 1773), one of the first and most important documents of the German 'Storm and Stress' movement, and *The Sufferings of Young Werther* (1774), a novel written very much from the heart and which rapidly achieved international fame. The success of the latter drew an invitation from Prince Karl August, Duke of Weimar, to join him at the Weimar court, and after an initial period of occasionally rather irresponsible behaviour with the young Duke (who was aged only eighteen), Goethe started to become far more than simply a writer in residence, famous for radical literary experiment. Much to the initial opposition of the court, he began to devote himself increasingly to the management of the Duke's affairs, proving himself conscientious and effective, and eventually winning considerable trust. A strong, emotional, but as far as we can tell, platonic, relationship with Charlotte von Stein, wife of the Duke's Master of Horse, a woman seven years his senior, was to prove decisive in shaping a more settled and responsible attitude to life. Goethe was to spend most of the rest of his life in Weimar, and, over the years, involved himself in the improvement of the Duchy in areas as diverse as mining, road building and irrigation. He also found the time to pursue a variety of scientific studies, in anatomy, botany, geology and optics.

Possibly because he felt trapped by the many obligations created by his position, possibly because he felt ensnared by his relationship with Frau von Stein, and possibly because he felt full literary inspiration was no longer to be found in Weimar, Goethe secretly planned a trip to Rome. He departed in 1786 and was to travel in Italy for almost two years. The experience revitalized his literary activities, and he returned to Weimar a different man. It was at this stage that a far greater maturity of formulation entered his writing and that he began to make regular jottings which were to form the basis of later maxims. A second visit to Italy, in 1790, undertaken in a very different frame of mind, was to prove a disappointment to him, although it was to inspire verse epigrams, the best of which show that successful wrestling with form which is often characteristic of the maxims themselves (the *Venetian Epigrams*, a selection of which was first published in 1791).

Although Goethe returned refreshed from his Italian journeys, non-literary activity was soon to engulf him once more, and the period after the second Italian visit is often regarded as one of unease and isolation. Friendship with the younger dramatist and historian Schiller proved a source of comfort and inspiration, and although the latter's death in 1805 was a severe emotional blow, two great works were to follow in the years thereafter: the first part of *Faust* (1808), on which he had been working sporadically for over thirty years, and then his novel *Elective Affinities* (1809), which contained the first selection of his maxims. Works of his later years came more slowly, but love was to inspire further major achievements in poetry, while the fruits of his reflection were increasingly made public in periodicals and in his final novel, *Wilhelm Meister's Journeyman Years* (1821, 1829). At his death in 1832, Goethe was planning the publication of a collection of maxims; thanks to the tireless work of his secretary (and literary executor) Eckermann, some 600 of these appeared in 1833 under the title *Einzelheiten. Maximen und Reflexionen* (*Individual Items. Maxims and Reflections*), while a much fuller collection, also under the aegis of Eckermann, appeared in 1840 under the general title *Sprüche in Prosa* (*Sayings in Prose*). This formulation was to be rejected at a later stage by Max Hecker who, in 1907, used the phrase Goethe himself had given the largest folder of his maxims in 1822: '*Maximen und Reflexionen*'. The author would probably not have objected to such a dignified title for an ultimately complete collection of his maxims, although he had regularly used other terms, labelling one folder of miscellaneous scraps of paper '*Späne*' ('shavings') and another '*Gnomen*' ('gnomes'). The only ones for which he consistently used the term 'aphorisms' are nos. 1064–96.

The bulk of the maxims were composed after 1800, but throughout his life – and especially after the journey to Italy – Goethe had the habit of jotting down, often on whatever scrap of paper was available, any thought that seemed to him worthy of structured formulation. From time to time, over the years, a secretary would make a fair copy of these (sometimes casual) thoughts so that the author could survey them and consider how they might be used in the context of other work which was in progress at the time. As a result, some of Goethe's ideas on art and related subjects appeared in periodicals he himself published (*On Art and Antiquity*, 1818–27); ideas of a scientific nature appeared in his journals on morphology (*Periodical Issues on Morphology*, 1822) and on the Natural Sciences in general (*Periodical Issues on the Natural Sciences*, 1823); while insights of a more general nature found a place in the context of his fiction where, it is true, their relevance was not always apparent (as 'diary entries' by one of the central characters in *Elective Affinities*, and as wise remarks taken mainly from 'Makarie's Archive' in *Wilhelm Meister*). In periodicals and novels, therefore, more than half of Goethe's available supply of 'Maxims and Reflections' appeared in his lifetime (798 out of 1413).

Goethe probably regarded his reflections as miniature creative language events to be shared with his readers, reflecting the time- and life-sequence of his personal reactions. He did not see them as a specific collection of aphorisms, nor as anything as planned and as formal as the biblical Wisdom books; nor did he wish to see them presented under specific headings which would enable swift reference to his opinions on a variety of matters (a task readily undertaken by later compilers). *Maxims and Reflections* is thus best regarded as something of a Goethe 'reader', not as a repository for learned information or profound thought but, in the main, for the pleasure that can be taken in a carefully crafted formulation that is sometimes akin to poetry in its diction and rhythm. It is significant that Goethe's letters and his conversation are often comparable to the 'maxim and reflection' form, and this may be one reason why he took the trouble to structure and formulate his passing thoughts, to set them down in formalized shape for posterity. Quickly scribbling down ideas was actually a process in which Goethe had engaged since youth, when, as the creative impulse came, he would immediately commit his thoughts to paper, not hesitating to spring out of bed to do so. He could not postpone the artistic process, nor, in fact, could he anticipate it. He knew that when inspiration came it must be seized – it would otherwise be lost. And so maxims were created on the back of theatre programmes, visiting cards, on his own literary drafts, and even on bills. There are, however, disadvantages to seizing the moment in such a way, and they are commonly overlooked by those critics who are eager to see the mark of genius or of wisdom in all that the Great Man wrote: given the manner in which some of the maxims were composed, it is hardly surprising that not all of them are good ones; some are tedious; and some are actually borrowed from others. But the advantages of this method of composition are equally clear: by reacting creatively to so many events and situations – in his reading, his personal encounters, his daily work in the offices of the Weimar court and its administration, his scientific work and the correspondence that went with it – the enthusiasm of the thinker is regularly preserved and the writer provides a complete personal record of his views on such diverse issues as life and art, books and people, truth and error, experience and wisdom, nature and science.

In the maxims, we see not simply ideas, but, above all, the effort to *structure* the idea. The principle of creating form was one which Goethe elevated above all others. It recurs in a number of the maxims, but is put most forcefully in a letter to one of his closest friends, the musician and composer Zelter:

No one is prepared to grasp that, both in nature and in art, the sole and supreme process is to create form and structure. (30 October 1808)

Goethe had to formulate his ideas on the spot, as it were, and one by one, in sequence, in an ordered structure of words. One has the impression that he grappled with an idea in its prose formulation much in the way he would work to set the right form for a poem, a couplet in one of his verse dramas, or a rhymed apophthegm – and that this was for him a satisfying, indeed a necessary, way of giving an immediate outward aspect to what was going on in his mind at the time, more particularly in response to some reading, some personal encounter, some visual or emotional reaction or experience. Some maxims are clearly the product of such a single moment, while others have been shaped over a period of time. The form adopted is constantly changing. Some are short statements of apparently artless simplicity. Others consist of a short statement and the idea which arises from it. Some develop a point over several sentences. Some are questions; some are short dialogues; some state a point, some argue it, others demonstrate it. Most are positive, while a small number are negative. Goethe will move from a single terse clause to a succession of complex sentences. He will move from solemnity to wit. Yet all the maxims share one aim: to provoke reflection.

Goethe used a variety of words to refer to his writings in short form, but 'maxims' was one of the most common. He would seem to have understood by the term a general truth as he personally saw it and wanted to communicate in crisp formulation; a 'reflection' was quite simply a rather more developed 'maxim'. Probably because his ideas had such a strongly personal context, Goethe tended to avoid the term 'aphorism', which, as R. J. Hollingdale has suggested in the Introduction to his Penguin collection of Lichtenberg's aphorisms, may be seen as distinguished by four qualities occurring together: it is brief, it is isolated, it is witty, and it is 'philosophical' (p. 9). Goethe's maxims only occasionally fulfil these criteria. They are not always brief, and they are often in a sequence rather than being isolated. Wit, one feels, is far less important to Goethe than veracity. Nor was he trying to solve intellectual problems or to make clever points. He did not see himself writing in the manner of Lichtenberg (whom he had met and whose work he admired), nor in that of the French seventeenth-century aphorists, such as La Rochefoucauld and Pascal, even though later critics have tended to place him in this tradition. His thinking and his subsequent formulation were always personal, independent and clear. Elements of paradox and ambiguity, which some have also claimed for the true aphorism, are rarely to be found here. Maxim 81 illustrates clearly what might be seen as a working principle:

Surely the world is quite full enough of riddles for us not to need to turn the simplest phenomena into riddles too?

Yet Goethe did, at the same time, want to preserve a certain (élitist) status for his thinking. In one of the two entries which actually refer to the business of writing maxims, he suggests (in no. 1068):

The obscurity of certain maxims is only relative: it doesn't do to make everything that is obvious to a practitioner crystal-clear to a listener.

Generalization on the maxims is difficult, because a loosely ordered sequence of disparate ideas, produced in reaction to a wide range of events, obviously resists broad analysis. Even deciding on the different groups into which the maxims can be placed is problematic, and Goethe himself is of limited assistance here. In one of his final conversations with his secretary Eckermann, the discussion turned to the '*Maximen und Reflexionen*' in *Wilhelm Meister* (conversation of 29 May 1831). Eckermann here recalls the way in which maxims had been introduced into the novel, which Goethe had earlier been revising for a new edition of his works. The author had expected the final product to take up three volumes, but when the printers pointed out that he had miscalculated and more material was needed, Goethe simply requested Eckermann to make up the necessary space out of two bundles of maxims which had not yet been published, while he himself added two recently composed poems. In the same conversation Goethe expressed the wish that poems and maxims be removed from later editions of *Wilhelm Meister*, and that at some point in the future the maxims as a whole be published in three groups relating to 'Art', 'Natural Sciences in General' and 'Literature and Ethics'. In view of the breadth of such categories, it is not surprising that later editors have seen fit to introduce further divisions. There have been careful, reasoned attempts not only to present the maxims in categories, themes and logical connections, but also to follow what has been seen as Goethe's circular and symbolical thinking. The resultant groupings are indeed very useful as an indication to the reader of the main areas of Goethe's thought, but such collections are unrepresentative of the process and of the unsystematic nature of Goethe's loose, day-by-day thoughts. Such editors presuppose that presentation should be by subject, but there is obviously a strong body of opinion which holds that chronology (in as far as this can be reasonably determined) is a more legitimate way of proceeding. This is, in fact, the principle adopted in the present version.

Further Reading

There have been a number of English translations of selected maxims. The first general collection was that by Bailey Saunders, *The Maxims and Reflections of Goethe* (1893, some 590 translated), while one of the best is that by Hermann J. Weigand, a selection by subject from all Goethe's late prose, including letters and conversations: *Wisdom and Experience. Selections* by Ludwig Curtius, translated and edited, with an introduction, by Hermann J. Weigand (Routledge & Kegan Paul, London, 1949). A 'parallel text' representative sample (159 maxims), together with introduction and notes, has been produced by Roger Stephenson (*Goethe's 'Maximen und Reflexionen'. A Selection*, Scottish Papers in Germanic Studies 8, Glasgow, 1986). Douglas Miller translates some sixty-two in vol. 12 of the Suhrkamp translation of Goethe's works (Suhrkamp, New York, 1988). Obviously, the maxims in *Elective Affinities* have been translated on regular occasions, most recently by R. J. Hollingdale (Penguin Classics, 1971), and David Constantine (World's Classics, 1994). Those in *Wilhelm Meister's Journeyman Years* have been translated less often. The best rendering is that by Krishna Wilson in the Suhrkamp translation, vol. 10 (Suhrkamp, New York, 1989).

The first serious studies were those by Bailey Saunders (the lengthy Preface to his selection) and by Max Hecker (the Introduction to his edition of 1907). Of more recent investigations, C. P. Magill's general essay remains one of the best surveys of the collection, although, as he points out, only a few of the maxims fit the title he uses, 'The Dark Sayings of the Wise: Some Observations on Goethe's *Maximen und Reflexionen*', *Publications of the English Goethe Society*, 36 (1965–6), 60–82. Roger Stephenson's full and excellent study, *Goethe's Wisdom*

Literature. A Study in Aesthetic Transformation (Peter Lang, Berne, Frankfurt, New York, 1983) surveys Goethe's Wisdom literature as a whole; the most relevant parts of this are reproduced in the Introduction to his *Selection* mentioned above. Stephenson is especially helpful in analysing what he calls the 'rhetorical form' of the maxims and in discussing their content. There is a good Introduction and detailed commentary on individual maxims in the 'Münchener Ausgabe' of Goethe's works, vol. 17, edited Gonthier-Louis Fink *et al.* (Carl Hanser, Munich, 1991), while the 'Frankfurter Ausgabe', edited by Harald Fricke (Deutscher Klassiker Verlag, Frankfurt am Main, 1993) contains the most exhaustive commentary yet published.

A Note on the Text

Since Goethe himself did not oversee the publication of his maxims as a separate volume, there has been much dispute over what precisely should be included in such a collection and in what order it should appear. The maxims featured in this volume first appeared scattered throughout the sixty-volume edition of Goethe's complete works edited by Eckermann and Riemer (Stuttgart, 1827–30; 1832–42), while later nineteenth-century editions adopted a variety of procedures for classifying them. In 1907 Max Hecker published them as a complete sequence, the first part of his volume being devoted to those published in Goethe's lifetime, arranged chronologically by date of publication, and the second to those which were among his unpublished papers. Paul Stöcklein followed this arrangement for the relevant volume of the 'Gedenkausgabe' (Zürich, 1949), which has been made widely available in paperback by the Deutscher Taschenbuch Verlag (Munich, 1963). The text in the popular Goethe 'Hamburger Ausgabe' (C. H. Beck, Munich, vol. 12, originally edited by H. J. Schrimpf in 1953, but with critical apparatus regularly revised) operated by grouping the maxims into eight different subject areas, and more recent editions have also chosen to deviate from Hecker's arrangement (the 'Münchener Ausgabe' and the 'Frankfurter Ausgabe', both mentioned above in 'Further Reading'). There have been recent reprints (with minor corrections) of Hecker's version, the latest being edited by Irmtraut Schmidt, with an introduction by Walther Killy (C. H. Beck, Munich, 1989).

Familiarity with the collection as a whole confirms the value of presenting the text in the traditional way thought out by Hecker on the basis of the manuscripts and of a judicious appraisal of the original editors, who had been, after all, in close touch with Goethe himself and who respected his own, personal ordering of certain well-defined groups – especially those in *Art and Antiquity* and in the two novels. The order in which the various sections are presented is less important than the order of the maxims within each individual group: there is often a sequence of thought, the development of an argument from one maxim to the next, and this is destroyed by grouping the items by subject. In addition, though, there is often the problem of deciding into which group certain items should be placed. It would, of course, be possible, and it has in fact been done (e.g. by Fink and Fricke), to add further items to the collection – from a variety of Goethe's other literary and non-literary works. But one can argue that the process need not end there, for Goethe's conversations, and also his letters, are thronged with possible candidates for inclusion. Goethe himself actually drew some of the maxims from these sources, and the process could easily be extended.

Goethe occasionally also borrowed from others, although he was not consistent in providing quotation marks to identify other people's words – indeed, he was once accused of plagiarism for failing to do so. However, not all of his sources are known. (Those that have been identified are mentioned in the Notes.)

The present translation was begun before the editions of Fink and Fricke had reached print, and although it is possible that the latter's will come to be recognized as definitive, justification for following the original Hecker presentation can comfortably be made; apart from the grounds outlined above, this text has acquired canonical status, its numbering is acknowledged, even if not followed, in all collections, and it is readily available in German paperback for those who wish to compare translation and original.

Maxims and Reflections

FROM *ELECTIVE AFFINITIES* (1809)

From Ottilie's Diary

1. We enjoy looking into the future because, by our secret longings, we so much want to bring about a favourable realization of the vague possibilities that move to and fro in that realm.

2. It is not easy for us to be in the company of many people without thinking that chance, having brought together so many, should also bring us our friends.

3. However secluded our life, sooner or later and without realizing it, we will find ourselves in debt or in credit.

4. If we meet someone who owes us thanks, it will immediately occur to us. How often we can meet someone where the debt is on our side, and we do not give it a thought!

5. To communicate is natural; to accept what is communicated is an acquired art.

6. No one would talk much in company if he realized how often he himself misunderstands others.

7. The reason, maybe, for our altered account of what others have said is our own failure to understand them.

8. Anyone who holds forth at length and without flattering his listeners will court dislike.

9. Every spoken word evokes its contrary meaning.

10. Contradiction and flattery both make for poor conversation.

11. The most congenial social occasions are those ruled by cheerful deference of each for all.

12. The clearest indication of character is what people find laughable.

13. What is laughable results from a moral contrast which has been put across for the senses in a harmless way.

14. Sensuous man often laughs where there is nothing to laugh at. Whatever stimulates him, his inner contentment shows itself.

15. The man who understands finds almost everything laughable, the man of reason practically nothing.

16. A man well on in years was taken to task for still paying attention to young women. 'It's the only way,' he replied, 'to rejuvenate oneself, and surely that's what everybody wants.'

17. We suffer people to tell us about our shortcomings, we condone punishment, we patiently endure a good deal on their account; but we are impatient when we are urged to discard them.

18. Certain shortcomings are necessary for an individual's existence. We would feel uncomfortable if old friends were to discard certain characteristics.

19. 'He'll soon die', as the saying goes, when someone acts out of character.

20. What kind of shortcomings are we allowed to keep, indeed cultivate in ourselves? The kind that flatter, rather than hurt, other people.

21. Passions are faults or virtues, only heightened ones.

22. Our passions are a genuine phoenix. As the old one burns down, the new one immediately arises out of the ashes.

23. Great passions are maladies without hope. What might heal them only makes them really dangerous.

24. Passion is both heightened and relieved by avowal. Maybe there is nothing where a middle way would be more desirable than in confiding and keeping silent *vis-à-vis* those we love.

25. It is the way of the world to accept a person as he presents himself; but he does have to present himself. We would rather tolerate a difficult person than suffer one who is insignificant.

26. One can foist anything on society, except what will have consequences.

27. We don't get to know people when they come to us. We have to go to them to discover how things stand.

28. I find it almost natural that we have all manner of things to criticize about visitors, and that when they leave we judge them not all that charitably; for in a way we have a right to measure them by our own standards. In such cases even sensible and fair-minded people can hardly refrain from sharp censure.

29. If we, however, have been visiting others and have seen them in their setting, in their ways, in their necessary unavoidable circumstances, how they operate or how they fit in, then we really must be obtuse and malevolent if we find laughable what in more senses than one should appear venerable.

30. What we call good conduct and manners is meant to achieve what could otherwise only be effected by force, or not even by force.

31. Association with women is the basic element of good manners.

32. How can a person's character and individuality go along with good manners?

33. Individuality should actually be heightened by good manners. Importance is what everybody wants, but it is not to be disturbing.

34. A well-educated soldier has the greatest advantages in life as a whole as well as in society.

35. Crude warriors at least don't deny their own character, and because kindness is usually hidden under their strength, it is even possible, if need be, to get on with them.

36. No one is more objectionable than an awkward civilian. As he is not forced to deal with crude matters, one could demand refinement from him.

37. Confident friendliness, where an attitude of reverence is indicated, is always laughable. No one would put down his hat when he has hardly got through his compliments if he realized how funny that looks.

38. There is no such thing as an outward gesture of courtesy unrelated to a profound moral motive. True education would be of a kind to pass on this gesture together with its motive.

39. Behaviour is a mirror in which everyone shows his image.

40. There is a courtesy of the heart; it is akin to love. From it comes the most comfortable courtesy of outward behaviour.

41. Voluntary dependence is the best of all states to be in, and how could this be possible without love!

42. We are never further away from our desires than when we imagine we possess what we desire.

43. No one is more a slave than the one who thinks he is free without being free.

44. A person has only to say he is free and he immediately feels constrained. If he has the courage to say he is constrained, then he feels free.

45. In the face of another's great excellence the only possible salvation is love.

46. There is something horrifying about a man of outstanding excellence of whom stupid people are proud.

47. There is no hero, it is said, for a valet-de-chambre. But this is only because a hero can only be recognized and appreciated by another hero. So the valet will probably be able to evaluate his equals at their true worth.

48. There is no greater consolation for mediocrity than the fact that genius is not immortal.

49. The greatest people are always linked with their century through some weakness.

50. One usually considers people more dangerous than they actually are.

51. Fools and intelligent people are equally undamaging. Half-fools and half-sages, these are the most dangerous of all.

52. There is no way of more surely avoiding the world than by art, and it is by art that you form the surest link with it.

53. Even at the moment of highest bliss and of highest distress we need the artist.

54. Art deals with what is hard to bear and with what is good.

55. Seeing difficulties handled with ease gives us a sight of the impossible.

56. Difficulties increase the nearer we get to the goal.

57. Sowing is not as onerous as harvesting.

FROM *ART AND ANTIQUITY*

Vol. I, issue 3: *Naïvety and Humour* (1818)

58. Art is a serious business, most serious of all when it deals with noble sacred subjects; but the artist stands above art and above the subject: above the former because he uses it for his purposes, above the latter because he treats it in his own personal way.

59. Plastic art has to rely entirely on what is visible, on the outer appearance of what is natural. The purely natural we describe as 'naïve' in so far as it is morally pleasing. Naïve subjects, therefore, are the domains of art which should be a moral expression of what is natural. Subjects which point in both directions are therefore the most auspicious.

60. What is naïve, being natural, is cognate to reality. Reality, devoid of any moral aspect, is what we term common.

61. Art is in itself noble; that is why the artist has no fear of what is common. This, indeed, is already ennobled when he takes it up, and so we see the greatest artists boldly exerting their personal right of majesty.

62. In every artist there is a potential foolhardiness without which talent is inconceivable; this is more particularly activated when there is an attempt to constrain a gifted man and to hire his services in one-sided ways.

63. And here, too, Raphael is probably the most pure among newer artists. He is altogether naïve, in his art reality is not in conflict with what is moral or even sacred. The tapestry depicting the Adoration of the Kings is a quite extraordinarily brilliant composition; from the most aged prince paying homage right down to the Moors and the monkeys mounted on camels and enjoying apples, Raphael depicts a whole world. Here, too, St Joseph could be characterized quite naïvely as the foster-father who is happy about the presents that have come in.

64. Artists, in general, have it in for St Joseph. The Byzantines, who cannot be accused of displaying too much humour, always make the saint look morose in nativity scenes. The child is bedded in the cradle, the animals look in, amazed that instead of their dry fodder they find a living creature of heavenly charm. Angels venerate the new arrival, his mother sits by quite still; but St Joseph sits facing the other way, turning his head crossly towards the strange scene.

65. Humour is one of the constituent elements of genius, but as soon as it predominates, it is no more than its surrogate; it goes hand in hand with art in decline and in the end destroys and annihilates it.

66. A work we now have in hand can explain this agreeably, the idea being to consider exclusively from an ethical point of view all those artists already known to us in various other ways, to expound by means of the subjects and the treatment of their works just what time and place, nation and teacher, what each artist's indestructible individuality has contributed towards fashioning them into what they became and keeping them to what they were.

Vol. II, issue 3: *Matters of Serious Moment* (1820)

67. Quite often, as life goes on, when we feel completely secure as we go on our way, we suddenly notice that we are trapped in error, that we have allowed ourselves to be taken in by individuals, by objects, have dreamt up an affinity with them which immediately vanishes before our waking eye; and yet we cannot tear ourselves away, held fast by some power that seems incomprehensible to us. Sometimes, however, we become fully aware and realize that error as well as truth can move and spur us on to action. Now because action is always a decisive factor, something really good can result from an active error, because the effect of all that has been done reaches out into infinity. So although creative action is certainly always best, destroying what has been done is also not without happy consequence.

68. But the strangest error is that relating to ourselves and to our potential so that we devote our efforts to a worthy task, an honourable enterprise which is beyond our scope, reaching out for a goal we can never attain. Everyone feels the resulting Tantalus-Sisyphus torment the more bitterly the more upright has been his intention. And yet, very often when we see ourselves for ever separated from what we had intended to achieve, we have already, on our way, found something else worth desiring, something conforming to our nature with which we were, in fact, born to rest content.

Vol. III, issue 1: *Own and Adopted Ideas in Proverbial Formulation* (1821)

69. If a person is to achieve all that others demand of him, he must consider himself more than he actually is.

70. As long as this isn't taken to absurd lengths, we are quite happy to put up with it.

71. Work makes the journeyman.

72. Certain books are apparently written not so that we may learn from them, but to demonstrate the fact that the author knew something.

73. They whip up curds hoping it might turn into cream.

74. It is easier to imagine the mental state of a man who labours under total error than the state of mind of someone deluding himself with half-truths.

75. Germans take pleasure in art that is unsure of itself and this stems from the fact that they are dabblers; for a dabbler cannot allow good art to be valid, else he himself would be worth nothing at all.

76. It is sad to watch an outstandingly talented man battling frantically with himself, his circumstances, his time, without ever managing to get anywhere. Sad instance: Bürger.

77. The greatest respect an author can have for his public is never to produce what is expected but what he himself considers right and useful for whatever stage of intellectual development has been reached by himself and others.

78. Wisdom is to be found only in truth.

79. I make a mistake and everyone can spot it; I tell a lie and no one knows.

80. The German is free in his thinking and that is why he fails to notice when he lacks freedom in matters of taste and of the spirit.

81. Surely the world is quite full enough of riddles for us not to need to turn the simplest phenomena into riddles too?

82. The smallest hair casts its shadow.

83. Whatever I have tried to do in the past by false tendencies I have in the end learnt to understand.

84. Open-handedness wins favour for each and everyone, especially if humility goes with it.

85. A last violent cloud of dust whirls round once before a thunderstorm, soon to be stilled for a long time.

86. It is not easy for people to know one another, even with the best will and determination; for, moreover, there is bad will, which distorts everything.

87. If people did not always want to put themselves on a par with others, they would know one another better.

88. Outstanding people are therefore in a worse case than others; as we don't compare ourselves with them, we try to catch them out.

89. It's not important in this world to know what people are like, but to be cleverer, at any given moment, than the person confronting us: witness all fairs and quacks.

90. One doesn't find frogs wherever there is water; but there is water where you hear frogs.

91. Anyone who doesn't know foreign languages knows nothing of his own.

92. A mistaken idea is all very well as long as you are young; but it's no good dragging it on into old age.

93. All false attitudes which age and linger on are useless, rancid stuff.

94. Through Cardinal Richelieu's despotic unreasonableness Corneille had lost faith in himself.

95. Nature happens on specifications as one might wander into a cul-de-sac: there is no way through and no desire to turn back; hence the stubborn persistence of national characteristics.

96. Metamorphosis in a higher sense of taking and giving, winning and losing, was already aptly described by Dante.

97. Everyone has some trait in his nature which, openly admitted, might well cause displeasure.

98. When a man reflects on his physical or moral state, he usually decides that he is ill.

99. Human nature needs to be numbed from time to time, but without being put to sleep; hence smoking, spirits, opiates.

100. What matters to an active man is to do the right thing; whether the right thing comes to pass should not bother him.

101. Some people keep knocking at the wall with a hammer and imagine they are hitting the nail on the head every time.

102. French words are not derived from written Latin words, but from spoken ones.

103. Events which are real by chance and in which, for the moment, we can discover neither a law of nature nor one of freedom may be termed common.

104. Painting and tattooing the body is a return to animality.

105. Writing up history is one way of getting rid of the past.

106. What you don't understand, you don't possess.

107. Not everyone to whom we pass on a striking insight uses it productively; he may take it as a quite well-known truth.

108. Favour, as a symbol of sovereignty, is bestowed by weak people.

109. There is nothing common which fails to look comic when put grotesquely.

110. Everyone manages to have just about enough strength left to act according to his convictions.

111. Let memory fail as long as our judgement remains intact when needed.

112. Natural poets, so-called, are fresh and newly arraigned talents, rejects of an over-cultivated, over-mannered and halting artistic epoch. They cannot avoid the commonplace, so one can view them as retrograde; they are, however, agents of regeneration and they give rise to new progress.

113. No nation attains the power of judgement until it can sit in judgement on itself. But this great advantage is attained very late in the day.

114. Instead of contradicting my words, people should act according to my ideas.

115. Nature grows dumb when subjected to torture; the true answer to honest questioning is yes! yes! no! no! All else is idle and basically evil.

116. People are put out because truth is so simple; they should remember that even so they still find it hard enough to use and apply truth for their own profit.

117. I curse those who create a private world of error and yet incessantly demand that man should be useful.

118. A school of thought is to be viewed as a single individual who talks to himself for a hundred years and is quite extraordinarily pleased with himself, however silly he may be.

119. A false doctrine cannot be refuted because it is, of course, based on the conviction that false is true. But one can, may, and indeed must, again and again, stress the opposite truth.

120. Take two little sticks and paint one red, the other blue, then immerse them in water next to one another and each will appear broken. Everyone can see this simple experiment with his own bodily eyes; one who views it with the eyes of the spirit will be set free from a thousand and more than a thousand erroneous paragraphs.

121. All who set themselves up against an ingenious cause are just striking against coals; sparks fly and kindle where they would otherwise have had no effect.

122. Man would not be the most distinguished being on earth were he not too distinguished for it.

123. What was discovered long ago is buried again; how hard Tycho tried to show that comets were regular structures, a fact known to Seneca long ago.

124. How long the to and fro argument about the Antipodes went on!

125. Certain minds have to be left to their private illusions.

126. It is possible for people to produce works which are null and void without being bad; null and void because they lack substance, not bad, because the writer's mind is informed by a general pattern of good models.

127. Snow is a fictitious cleanliness.

128. He who is afraid of ideas in the end also lacks concepts.

129. We rightly describe as our masters those from whom we can go on learning. Not everyone from whom we learn deserves this title.

130. All that is lyrical must be very reasonable as a totality, and in its detail a little bit unreasonable.

131. There is something in your general make-up which is rather like the sea, to which we give a variety of names – and in the end it's all just salt water.

132. The saying has it that conceited self-praise stinks; that may well be true, but the public has no nose for the kind of smell that goes with unjust censure by outsiders.

133. The novel is a subjective epic in which the author begs permission to describe the world in his own way. So the only question is: does he have a way? – the rest will come in due course.

134. There are problematic natures not up to coping with any situation in which they find themselves and to whom none does justice. This is the source of the tremendous inner conflict which consumes life without giving any joy.

135. Our really and truly good deeds are mostly done *clam, vi et precario* [in secret, with great effort and precariously].

136. A merry companion is like a cart to give us a lift as we wander along on our way.

137. Dirt glitters when the sun happens to shine.

138. The miller thinks that no wheat grows except to keep his mill going.

139. It is difficult to be tolerant about the present moment: an indifferent one bores us, a good one has to be carried, and a bad one dragged.

140. The happiest man is one who can link the end of his life with its beginning.

141. People are so obstinately contradictory: they dislike being urged to their advantage, they put up with any amount of constraint to their disadvantage.

142. Circumspection is simple, later hindsight is complex.

143. A state of affairs which leads to daily vexation is not the right state.

144. Nothing is more usual in the case of uncautious behaviour than looking around for possible escape routes.

145. Hindus in the desert vow never to eat fish.

146. A partial truth goes on working for a time, but then, instead of complete enlightenment, a dazzling error suddenly intrudes; the world makes do with that and in this way whole centuries are duped.

147. In the sciences it is very worthwhile to seek out and then develop a partial truth already possessed by the Ancients.

148. Opinions tentatively broached are like counters moved forward in a board game; they may be defeated, but they have set in motion a game that will be won.

149. It is as certain as it is wonderful that truth and error spring from the same source; frequently, therefore, error must not be attacked because this would also mean attacking the truth.

150. Truth belongs to man, error to time. This is why it was said about an extraordinary man: '*Le malheur des temps a causé son erreur, mais la force de son âme l'en a fait sortir avec gloire.*' ['The misery of the times caused his error but the strength of his soul delivered him from it with glory.']

151. Everyone has his idiosyncrasies and cannot get rid of them; and yet quite a few people are destroyed by their idiosyncrasies, often by the most innocent ones.

152. A person who doesn't rate himself too highly is worth much more than he imagines.

153. In art and in learning as in deeds and action, everything depends on the fact that objects are understood clearly and treated according to their nature.

154. If reasonable, thoughtful people have a low opinion of the sciences in old age, this is only because they have demanded too much both of science and of themselves.

155. I'm sorry for people who make a great to-do about the transitory nature of things and get lost in meditations on earthly nothingness. Surely we are here precisely so as to turn what passes into something that endures; but this is only possible if you can appreciate both.

156. One phenomenon, one experiment, cannot prove anything; it is the link in a great chain, only valid in its context. If someone were to cover up a string of pearls and only show the most beautiful one, expecting us to believe that all the rest were like that, it is very unlikely that anyone would risk the deal.

157. Illustrations, verbal description, measurement, number and sign still do not constitute a phenomenon. The only reason why Newton's doctrine could survive for so long is that this error was embalmed for a couple of centuries in the quarto volume of the Latin translation.

158. One must repeat one's confession of faith from time to time, actually state what one condones, what one condemns; for the opposing camp isn't silent either.

159. At the present time no one should be silent or give in; we must talk and be up and doing, not in order to vanquish, but so as to keep on the alert; whether with the majority or the minority is a matter of indifference.

160. What the French describe as '*tournure*' is presumption with a look of charm. This makes us realize that Germans cannot have '*tournure*'; their arrogance is hard and harsh, their charm mild and humble; the one excludes the other and the two cannot be combined.

161. When a rainbow has lasted as long as a quarter of an hour we stop looking at it.

162. It used to happen, and still does, that I dislike a work of art because I'm not up to appreciating it; but if I sense some merit there, I try to get at it and this often leads to the happiest discoveries: new qualities are revealed to me in these things, new capacities in myself.

163. Faith is a secret capital sum in one's own home just as there are public savings and trust banks where individuals are supplied in days of need; here the creditor himself takes up his interest.

164. However ordinary life may look, however readily it appears to put up with what is common, everyday, it yet goes on secretly nursing higher demands and looks round for ways of satisfying them.

165. Real obscurantism doesn't operate by blocking the spread of what is true, clear and useful, but by circulating and validating what is false.

Vol. IV, issue 2: *Own and Assimilated Material* (1823)

166. It is much easier to recognize error than to find truth; the former lies on the surface, this is quite manageable; the latter resides in depth, and this quest is not everyone's business.

167. We all live on the past and perish by the past.

168. When we are called to learn something great, we at once take refuge in our native poverty and yet have still learnt something.

169. The Germans are indifferent about staying together, yet they do want to be on their own. Each person, never mind who he may be, has his own way of being alone and is unwilling to be deprived of this.

170. The empirical-moral world consists largely of bad will and envy.

171. Superstition is the poetry of life; so it does the poet no harm to be superstitious.

172. Trust is a curious matter. Listen only to one person: he may be wrong or deceiving himself; listen to many: they are in the same case, and as a rule you don't really discover the truth.

173. One should not wish anyone disagreeable conditions of life; but for him who is involved in them by chance, they are touchstones of character and of the most decisive value to man.

174. A limited, honest man often sees right through the knavery of the sharpest tricksters.

175. One who feels no love must learn to flatter, otherwise he won't make out.

176. You can neither protect nor defend yourself against criticism; you have to act in defiance of it and this is gradually accepted.

177. The crowd cannot do without efficient people and always finds efficiency burdensome.

178. Anyone who tells on my faults is my master, even if it happens to be my servant.

179. Memoirs from above downwards, or from below upwards: they are always bound to meet.

180. If you demand duties from people and will not concede them rights, you have to pay them well.

181. When a landscape is described as romantic, this means that there is a tranquil sense of the sublime in the form of the past, or, what amounts to the same, of solitude, remoteness, seclusion.

182. The splendid liturgical song '*Veni Creator Spiritus*' is in actual fact a call addressed to genius; and this is also why it appeals powerfully to people who are spirited and strong.

183. Beauty is a manifestation of secret natural laws which without this appearance would have remained eternally hidden from us.

184. I can promise to be candid, not, however, to be impartial.

185. Ingratitude is always a kind of weakness. I have never known competent people to be ungrateful.

186. We are all so blinkered that we always imagine we are right; and so we can imagine an extraordinary spirit, a person who not only makes a mistake but even enjoys being wrong.

187. Completely moderate action to achieve what is good and right is very rare; what we usually see is pedantry seeking to retard, impertinence seeking to precipitate.

188. Word and image are correlatives which are always in quest of one another as metaphors and comparisons show us clearly enough. Thus, from of old, what is inwardly said or sung for the ear is at the same time intended for the eye. And so in ages which seem to us childlike, we see in codes of law and salvational doctrine, in bible and in primer, a continual balance of word and image. If they put into words what did not go into images, or formed an image of what could not be put into words, that was quite proper; but people often went wrong about this and used the spoken word instead of the pictorial image, which was the origin of those doubly wicked symbolically mystical monsters.

189. Anyone who devotes himself to the sciences suffers, firstly through retardations and then through preoccupations. To begin with, people are reluctant to admit the value of what we are providing; later on they act as though they already knew what we might be able to provide.

190. A collection of anecdotes and maxims is the greatest treasure for a man of the world – as long as he knows how to weave the former into apposite points of the course of conversation, and to recall the latter on fitting occasions.

191. People say, 'Artist, study nature!' But it is no small matter to develop what is noble out of what is common, beauty out of what lacks form.

192. Where concern is lost, memory fares likewise.

193. The world is a bell that is cracked: it clatters, but does not ring out clearly.

194. One must put up kindly with the pressing overtures of young dilettantes: with age they become the truest votaries of art and of the master.

195. When people really deteriorate, their only contribution is malicious joy in the misfortune of others.

196. Intelligent people are always the best encyclopaedia.

197. There are people who never make mistakes because they never have sensible projects.

198. Knowing my attitude to myself and to the world outside me is what I call truth. And so everyone can have his own truth and yet it remains the self-same truth.

199. What is particular is eternally defeated by what is general; the general has eternally to fit in with the particular.

200. No one can control what is really creative, and everybody just has to let it go its own way.

201. Anyone to whom nature begins to unveil its open mystery feels an irresistible yearning for nature's noblest interpreter, for art.

202. Time is itself an element.

203. Man never understands how anthropomorphic he is.

204. A difference which gives reason nothing to register is not a difference.

205. In phanerogamy there is still so much of what is cryptogamic that centuries will not suffice to unriddle it.

206. Exchanging one consonant for another might perhaps be due to some organ deficiency, transforming a vowel into a diphthong the result of conceited pathos.

207. If one had to study all laws, one would have no time at all to transgress them.

208. One can't live for everyone, more especially not for those with whom one wouldn't care to live.

209. A call to posterity originates in the clear vital feeling that there is such a thing as permanence and that even if this is not immediately acknowledged it will, in the end, win the recognition of a minority and finally of a majority.

210. Mysteries do not as yet amount to miracles.

211. I convertiti stanno freschi appresso di me. [The converted are puzzled by me.]

212. Reckless, passionate favouritism of problematic men of talent was a failing of my younger years of which I could never completely rid myself.

213. I would like to be honest with you without us parting company; but this isn't possible. You are acting wrongly and trying to sit between two stools, not getting any followers and losing your friends. What's to come of this!

214. No matter whether you're of high rank or low, you can't avoid paying the price of your common humanity.

215. Writers of a liberal persuasion are now on to a good game; they have the whole public at their feet.

216. When I hear talk about liberal ideas, I'm always amazed how people like to delude themselves with the sound of empty words: an idea is not allowed to be liberal! Let it be forceful, doughty, self-enclosed, so as to fulfil its God-given mission of being productive. Still less is a concept allowed to be liberal; for its commission is completely different.

217. But where we have to look for liberality is in people's attitudes and these are their feelings come to life.

218. Attitudes, however, are seldom liberal because an attitude springs directly from the person, his immediate context and his needs.

219. We'll leave it at that; by this yardstick we should measure what we hear day after day!

220. It's always only our eyes, the way we imagine things; nature quite alone knows what it wills, what it intended.

221.
        'Give me where I stand!'
           Archimedes.
        'Take where you stand!'
           Nose.
        Declare where you stand!
           G.

222. It is general causal relationships which the observer will explore, and he will attribute similar phenomena to a general cause; rarely will he think of the immediate cause.

223. No intelligent man experiences a minor stupidity.

224. In every work of art, great or small, and down to the smallest detail, everything depends on the initial conception.

225. There is no such thing as poetry without tropes as poetry is a single trope writ large.

226. A kindly old examiner whispers into a schoolboy's ear: '*Etiam nihil didicisti*' [you haven't learnt anything as yet] and gives him a pass-mark.

227. Excellence is unfathomable; tackle it in what way you will.

228. *Aemilium Paulum – virum in tantum landandum, in quantum intelligi virtus potest.* [Aemilius Paulus – a man to be praised as highly as virtue can be understood.]

229. I was intent on pursuing what is general until such time as I came to comprehend the achievement of outstanding people in what is particular.

Vol. V, issue 1: *Individual Points* (1824)

230. In the course of my long-standing interest in the life history of people of little and of great importance, I chanced on the following idea: you might compare the former with the warp in the world tapestry, the latter with the weft; the first really indicate the extent of the web in its width, the others its tension, firmness, with the addition, maybe, of some kind of pattern. But fate with its shears determines the length to which all else must yield and be subject. We won't pursue the comparison any further.

231. Books, too, have their life-experience which cannot be taken away from them.

> Who never ate his bread with tears,
> Who never sat weeping on his bed
> Through long nights of sorrow,
> He does not know you, O heavenly powers.

These deeply painful lines were said over to herself by a most perfect, adored queen, condemned to the cruellest exile and boundless banishment. She made a friend of the book which transmits these words and much other painful experience, drawing from it grievous comfort; who could dare to belittle an impact which even now reaches out into eternity?

232. It is of the greatest delight to see how, in the Apollo room of the Villa Aldobrandini in Frascati, Domenico has placed Ovid's Metamorphoses in the most fitting surroundings; and in this connection we like to remember that our experience of the most joyful events is doubly blissful if vouchsafed to us in a splendid landscape, indeed, that moments which were in themselves indifferent are raised to high significance by a worthy setting.

233. Poetry is most effective when things are beginning, be they altogether crude, half-cultured, or when a culture is in the process of change, when a foreign culture is being apprehended, so that one can say there is undeniably the effect of a new beginning.

234. In the seventeenth century one's female lover was aptly termed 'man-intoxicator'.

235. At Hiddensee the most loving expression is 'dear washed-clean little soul'.

236. Truth is a torch, but a monstrously huge one; which is why we are all just intent on getting past it, our eyes blinking as we go, even terrified of getting burnt.

237. 'Wise people have a lot in common' – Aeschylus.

238. The unreasonable thing about otherwise reasonable people is that they don't know how to sort out what someone is saying when he's not really put it as precisely as he should have done.

239. Because he speaks, everyone believes that he can also speak about language.

240. You've only got to grow old to be more lenient; I see no fault committed of which I too haven't been guilty.

241. The person engaged in action is always unconscionable; no one except the contemplative has a conscience.

242. Do happy people imagine that an unhappy person should perish decently before them like a gladiator as the Roman rabble used to demand?

243. Timon consulted someone about his children's education. 'Let them,' this man said, 'be taught matters they will never understand.'

244. There are people whom I wish well and would wish I could wish even better.

245. One brother broke pots, the other broke pitchers. Destructive goings-on!

246. Just as, out of habit, one consults a run-down clock as though it were still going, so too one may look at the face of a beautiful woman as though she were still in love.

247. Hatred is active displeasure, envy is passive; hence one need not be surprised that envy soon turns into hatred.

248. There is something magical about rhythm; it even makes us believe that the sublime is something of our own.

249. A dilettante who takes his subject seriously and a scholar who works mechanically turn into pedants.

250. Art can be furthered by no one except the master. Benefactors further the artist, that's right and proper; but that is not always the way art is furthered.

251. 'Clarity is a suitable distribution of light and shade.' Hamann, take note!

252. Shakespeare is rich in wonderful images which arise from personified concepts and would not become us at all, while, to him, they are wholly apposite, because in his time all art was dominated by allegory. The art of printing had been invented over a hundred years before, and still had an aura of sacredness, as we can tell from the way books were bound at that time, and thus the noble poet loved and honoured them. We, however, now stitch our paper covers and do not readily respect either the binding or the content of a book.

253. Herr von Schweinichen's [journal] is a remarkable record of history and of manners; we are richly rewarded for the trouble taken to read it. For certain conditions it can become a treasury of symbolism of the most perfect kind. It is not a 'reader', but it is essential to have read it.

254. It is the most foolish of all errors for young people of good intelligence to imagine that they will forfeit their originality if they acknowledge truth already acknowledged by others.

255. Scholars are usually hostile when they are refuting; someone who is wrong is immediately seen as a deadly enemy.

256. Beauty can never be clear about itself.

257. As soon as subjective and so-called sentimental poetry was given the same rights as objective, descriptive poetry – and this is something which could really not have been avoided, as it would have led to the complete rejection of modern poetry – it was to be expected that even if a true poetical genius appeared, he would always portray the cheerful aspects of the inner life rather than the general aspects of a great worldly life. This has in fact happened, so that there is no such thing as poetry without images and one cannot, of course, withhold all commendation.

Vol. V, issue 2: *Individual Points* (1825)

258. On the scaffold Madame Roland asked for writing materials so as to register the very special thoughts that came to her on her last journey. A pity she was denied this; for at the end of life ideas dawn on a composed mind that have till then been unthinkable; they are like blessed spirits that alight shining on the mountain summits of the past.

259. You often say to yourself in the course of your life that you ought to avoid having too much business, 'polypragmosyne', and, more especially, that the older you get, the more you ought to avoid entering on new business. But it's all very well saying this, and giving yourself and others good advice. The very fact of growing older means taking

up a new business; all our circumstances change, and we must either stop doing anything at all or else willingly and consciously take on the new role we have to play on life's stage.

260. Great talents are a rarity, and it is rare that such people recognize themselves for what they are; but vigorous unconscious action and thinking have such highly gratifying, but also ungratifying, results that a significant life may well be consumed in a conflict of this kind. Instances of this, as remarkable as they are sad, are provided by Medwin's conversations.

261. I don't venture to talk about the absolute in a theoretical sense; I may, however, be allowed to state that anyone who has seen and recognized it as a phenomenon and always kept it in view will experience very great gain.

262. To live in the realm of ideas means treating the impossible as though it were possible. The same goes for character: if the two coincide, events follow from which the world's astonishment takes centuries to recover.

263. Napoleon, who lived wholly in a realm of ideas, was, however, incapable of a conscious grasp of this realm; he completely repudiates everything ideological, in denying all reality while all the time eagerly intent on realizing it. But his clear, incorruptible intellect cannot bear a perpetual inner contradiction of this kind, and it is most important when he is, as it were, impelled to talk about this matter in a characteristic and most attractive way.

264. He looks on the idea as a spiritual being which, although it has no reality, does, when it disintegrates, leave behind a residuum (*caput mortuum*), the reality of which we cannot wholly deny. If this seems to us rigid and all too materialistic, he can also talk quite differently in trustful and confidential conversation with his friends about the irresistible consequences of his life and doings. Then he likes to admit that life brings forth what is alive, that thoroughly creative action has far-reaching effects for all time. He likes to admit that he has given fresh stimulus, a new direction to the course of the world.

265. However, it remains very remarkable that people whose personality is almost entirely 'idea' are so very shy of the realm of fantasy. Hamann was like this: it seemed intolerable to him to hear talk about things in another world than this. From time to time he gave expression to this dislike in a certain paragraph of which, however, he wrote fourteen variations, and even then probably being unsatisfied with what he had written. Two of these attempts have come down to us; we ourselves have ventured to formulate a third one which we are publishing by reason of our earlier reflections above.

266. Man is set as a reality in the midst of a real world and is endowed with organs of a kind capable of both recognizing and also producing what is real and at the same time possible. All healthy people are convinced of their own existence and of something that exists all around them. At the same time there is also a hollow spot in the brain, that is, a place where no object is mirrored, just as in the eye itself there is a little spot which has no vision. If a man devotes special attention to this place, if he immerses himself in it, he falls victim to a mental illness and here has an intuition about things in another world which are, in fact, non-entities, having neither form nor limit but which, like a void-in-the-night, instil fear and in more than ghostly fashion persecute those who do not vigorously tear themselves away.

267. How little of all that has happened has been recorded in writing, how little of this corpus of writings has been preserved! By its very nature, literature is fragmentary; it contains monuments of the human spirit in so far as these constitute written texts and have ultimately survived.

268. And yet, in spite of all the incompleteness of the literary scene, we find repetitions multiplied a thousandfold, which shows how limited are man's mind and his destiny.

269. As, however, we have been called upon to be assessors, though without a brief, of this general world council, and we allow ourselves to be briefed day in day out by newspaper journalists, it is also great luck to discover competent reporters about times past. In recent times I have found writers of this kind in Raumer and Wachler.

270. The question as to which of the two is greater, the historian or the poet, should not even be raised; they do not compete with one another, as little as does the runner with the boxer. To each is due his own crown.

271. The historian has a twofold duty: firstly towards himself and then to his reader. On his own account he must submit to precise scrutiny what might actually have happened, and for his reader's sake he must establish what in fact did happen. How he deals with his own attitude can be agreed with his colleagues; the public, however, must not be let into the secret of how little in history can be deemed to be definitely settled.

272. Books, we find, are like new acquaintances. To begin with, we are highly delighted if we find an area of general agreement, if we feel a friendly response concerning some important aspect of our life. It is only on closer acquaintance that differences begin to emerge, at which point the great thing is not immediately to recoil, as may happen at a more youthful age, but to cling very firmly to areas of agreement and fully to clarify our differences without on that account aiming at identity in our views.

273. Friendly and instructive entertainment of this kind was provided for me by Stiedenroth's *Psychology*. He is incomparably good in his exposition of the total effect of what is outside or what is within, and we gradually see the world created anew in ourselves. But he is not as successful in describing the contrary outward reaction of the inner world. He does less than justice to the entelechy which does not assimilate without also appropriating something of its own; and genius simply does not fit into this scheme; and in thinking he can derive the ideal from experience and saying: a child doesn't idealize, one could reply: a child doesn't procreate; for becoming aware of the ideal also presupposes a form of puberty. But enough of this, he remains a valued companion and friend and is always to be within reach.

274. Anyone who lives much among children will find that no impression made from outside remains without a counter-reaction.

275. The counter-reaction of a really childlike being is even passionate, its intervention firm.

276. That is why children live in a realm of hasty judgements, indeed, of prejudice; for time is needed to blot out what has been seized in one-sided haste and then replace it with something more general. To pay attention to this is one of the educator's chief duties.

277. A two-year-old boy had understood the fact of birthday celebrations and had accepted with joy and gratitude the presents received on his birthday, sharing, too, in his brother's pleasure when his turn came.

  As a result of this, when there were so many presents around on Christmas Eve, he asked when his Christmas would come. It took a whole further year for him to understand a general feast for all.

278. The great difficulty about psychological observations is that you always have to look on the inner and outer sphere as being parallel or, rather, as interwoven. There is constant systole and diastole, a breathing in and a breathing out of the living organism; even if you cannot actually pronounce on this, you must observe it precisely and bear it in mind.

279. My relationship with Schiller was based on the decisive bent of both of us towards one object; our shared activity rested on our differing ways of striving to achieve this object.

  On a slight disagreement between us which we once discussed and of which I am reminded by a passage in his letter, I made the following reflections.

  There is a great difference whether a poet is looking for the particular that goes with the general, or sees the general in the particular. The first gives rise to allegory where the particular only counts as an example, an illustration of the particular; but the latter in fact constitutes the nature of poetry, expressing something particular without any thought of the general, and without indicating it. Now whoever has this living grasp of the particular is at the same time in possession of the general, without realizing it, or else only realizing it later on.

280. The only way to see absurdities of the day in proportion is to compare them with great masses of world history.

Vol. V, issue 3: *Individual Points* (1826)

281. You really only know when you know little; doubt grows with knowledge.

282. It's really a person's mistakes that make him endearing.

283. *Bonus vir semper tiro.* [A good man is always a beginner.]

284. There are people who love and seek out those like themselves, and, then again, those who love and pursue their opposites.

285. Anyone who had always allowed himself to take so poor a view of the world as our adversaries make out would have turned into a rotten subject.

286. Envy and hatred limit the observer's view to the surface even if this is also associated with acumen; if this, however, goes hand in hand with kindliness and love, the observer can see right through the world and mankind; indeed, he can hope to reach the Allhighest.

287. An English critic credits me with 'panoramic ability', for which I must tender my most cordial thanks.

288. A certain measure of poetical talent is desirable for every German as the right way to cloak his condition, of whatever kind it may be, with a certain degree of worth and charm.

289. The subject-matter is visible to everyone, content is only discovered by him who has something to contribute, and form is a mystery to most.

290. People's inclinations favour what is vitally alive. And youth again forms itself by youth.

291. We may get to know the world however we choose, it will always keep a day and a night aspect.

292. Error is continually repeated in action, and that is why we must not tire of repeating in words what is true.

293. Just as in Rome, besides the Romans, there was also a people of statues, so, too, apart from this real world, there is also an illusory world, mightier almost, where the majority live.

294. People are like the Red Sea: the staff has hardly kept them apart, immediately afterwards they flow together again.

295. The historian's duty: to distinguish truth from falsehood, certainty from uncertainty, doubtful matters from those which are to be rejected.

296. Only someone to whom the present is important writes a chronicle.

297. Thoughts recur, convictions perpetuate themselves; circumstances pass by irretrievably.

298. Among all peoples, the Greeks have dreamt life's dream most beautifully.

299. Translators are to be regarded as busy matchmakers who exalt the great loveliness of a half-veiled beauty: they kindle an irresistible longing for the original.

300. We like to rate Antiquity higher than ourselves, but not posterity. It's only a father who doesn't envy a son's talent.

301. It's not at all hard to subordinate yourself; but when you are set on a declining course, in the descendant, how hard it is to admit that what is, in fact, below you is above you!

302. Our whole achievement is to give up our existence in order to exist.

303. All we devise and do is exhausting; happy the man who doesn't get weary.

304. 'Hope is the second soul of those who are unfortunate.'

305. '*L'amour est un vrai recommenceur.*' [Love is truly a new beginning.]

306. There is, too, in man a desire to serve; hence French chivalry is a form of service, '*servage*'.

307. 'In the theatre visual and aural entertainment greatly limit reflection.'

308. Experience can be extended into infinity; in not quite the same sense theory can be purified and perfected. To the former the universe is open in all directions; the latter remains locked within the confines of human capacity. This is why all modes of conceptual thinking are bound to reappear, and that is why, strangely enough, a theory of limited value can regain favour in spite of wider experience.

309. It is always the same world which lies open to our view, is always contemplated or surmised, and it is always the same people who live in truth or wrong-headedly, more comfortably in the latter way than in the former.

310. Truth is contrary to our nature, not so error, and this for a very simple reason: truth demands that we should recognize ourselves as limited, error flatters us that, in one way or another, we are unlimited.

311. It is now nearly twenty years since all Germans 'transcend'. Once they notice this, they are bound to realize how odd they are.

312. It is natural enough that people should imagine they can still do what they were once able to do; that others imagine themselves capable of doing what they never could do is perhaps strange but not infrequent.

313. At all times only individuals have had an effect on scientific knowledge, not the epoch. It was the epoch that did Socrates to death by poison, the epoch that burnt Huss: epochs have always remained true to type.

314. This is true symbolism, where the particular represents the general, not as dream and shadow, but as a live and immediate revelation of the unfathomable.

315. As soon as the ideal makes a demand on the real, it in the end consumes it and also itself. Thus credit (paper money) consumes silver and its own self.

316. Mastery is often seen as egoism.

317. As soon as good works and their merit cease, sentimentality immediately takes over in the case of Protestants.

318. If you can seek out good advice, it's as though you yourself have the capacity for action.

319. Mottoes point to what one hasn't got, what one is striving for. As is right and fitting, one keeps this constantly in view.

320. 'If you don't want to lift a stone on your own, you should leave it alone even when someone else is around.'

321. Despotism promotes autocracy because it expects a sense of responsibility in each individual, whether of elevated or low standing, and in this way evokes the highest degree of activity.

322. All that tends towards Spinoza in the poetical realm turns into Machiavellism in the area of reflection.

323. You have to pay dearly for your mistakes if you want to get rid of them, and even then you can count yourself lucky.

324. If a German writer wanted to lord it over his nation in olden days, all he had to do was to put across the idea that there was someone around who wanted to rule over them. Then people were forthwith so intimidated that they were glad to be bossed no matter by whom.

325. 'Nothing in the human situation is as unstable or fleeting as power not born of its own strength.'

326. There are also pseudo-artists: dilettanti and speculators; the former go in for art for the sake of pleasure, the latter for profit.

327. Sociability was part of my nature; and that is why I was able to enlist fellow workers for my manifold projects and make myself their fellow worker; in this way I had the good fortune to see myself live on in them, and them in me.

328. The sum total of my inner activity has turned out to be a lively process of trial and error, a heuristic process acknowledging an unknown intuitively surmised rule, an endeavour to find one of this kind in the outer world and introduce it into the outer world.

329. There is an enthusiastic way of reflecting which is of the greatest value, provided only that you don't let it carry you away.

330. Preparation for school is to be found only in the school itself.

331. Error is related to truth as sleeping is to waking. I have observed that when one has been in error, one turns to truth as though revitalized.

332. Everyone suffers who doesn't act for himself. One acts for others so as to share in their enjoyment.

333. What is conceivable belongs to the realm of the senses and the understanding. Adjoining this is propriety which is related to seemliness. Propriety, however, is a condition belonging to a particular time and to a definite set of circumstances.

334. We really only learn from books we cannot judge. The author of a book we could really judge ought surely to be learning from us.

335. That is why the Bible is an eternally effective book, because as long as the world goes on, no one will appear and say: I grasp it as a whole and understand it in detail. We, however, say modestly: as a whole it is venerable and in detail we can make use of it.

336. All mysticism is transcendence of and detachment from some object which one considers is being relinquished. The greater and the more meaningful what is given up, the richer the mystic's productions.

337. Oriental mystical poetry is at a great advantage in that the richness of the world, to which the initiate can point, is always available to the poet. This means that he is still at the very centre of the plenitude which he is leaving, and he revels in what he would like to discard.

338. Because religion itself offers mysteries, there ought not to be Christian mystics. They, moreover, rapidly become abstruse, tending towards the abyss of personal subjectivity.

339. A witty man says that the new kind of mysticism is the dialectic of the heart, and that what sometimes makes it so astonishing and seductive is that it raises to an articulate level matters not otherwise accessible by the usual avenues of understanding, reason and religion. Let anyone who believes he has enough courage and vigour to study it without being overwhelmed go down into the cavern of Trophonius, but do it at his own peril.

340. The Germans should not utter the word '*Gemüt*' for a span of thirty years and then '*Gemüt*' would gradually be forthcoming again; now it only signifies condoning our own and other people's foibles.

341. People's prejudices are based on the respective character of each individual, and that is why, closely associated as they are with this circumstance, they are altogether inseparable; neither clear evidence nor common sense nor reason have the slightest effect on them.

342. Character often makes a law out of weakness. People who are experts in the way of the world have said: 'Fear used as a mask for intelligence is insuperable.' Weak people often have revolutionary views; they imagine they would be happy if they were not subject to rule and don't feel that they are incapable of governing either themselves or others.

343. More recent German artists are precisely in the same case: they declare that the branch of art beyond their reach is doing damage and is therefore to be chopped off.

344. Common sense is born unalloyed in sound people, develops spontaneously and manifests itself in a definite realization and acknowledgement of what is necessary and useful. Practical men and women apply and use it with sound judgement. Where it is lacking, both sexes think that what they covet is necessary and what pleases them is useful.

345. All those who reach a state of freedom put across their failings: strong people exaggerate, weak people are negligent.

346. The battle of what is old, established, continuous against development, against further or against new formation, always remains the same. All order finally issues in pedantry; to get rid of the latter one destroys the former, and it takes a while before people realize that there has got to be a return to order. Classicism and Romanticism, domination by guilds and the demand for free trade, tenacious clinging to and shattering of basic foundations: it is always the same conflict which, in the end, always creates a new one. A ruler's most sensible procedure would therefore be to moderate this battle so that, without the destruction of any one side, it reaches a point of balance; but this isn't given to man and God doesn't seem to want it either.

347. Which training method is to be considered best? Answer: that of the natives of Hydra Island. Islanders and seafarers as they are, they soon take their boys on board ship and let them grow up in service. As soon as they achieve anything, they share in the spoils; and so they already take an interest in trade, barter and booty, and this forms the most competent coasters and seafarers, the most canny traders and the most audacious pirates. A basic group of this kind may of course nurture heroes who in their own person fix the destructive firebrand to the flagship of the enemy fleet.

348. Everything excellent limits us momentarily because we feel unable to match up to it; only in so far as we subsequently accept it into our own culture, absorb it as belonging to our own mental and temperamental powers, do we come to love and value it.

349. No wonder that we more or less prefer to be surrounded by mediocrity because it leaves us in peace; it gives us the cosy feeling of consorting with the likes of our own selves.

350. You don't have to censure vulgarity; for this remains eternally true to itself.

351. We cannot get away from a contradiction in our own make-up; we must make an effort to reconcile it. If other people contradict us, that's not our concern, that's their business.

352. There is at one and the same time so much capacity and excellence in the world, but no convergence between them.

353. You ask which form of government is the best? Whichever teaches us to govern ourselves.

354. You, a capable man, cannot instruct by lecturing; this, like preaching, is truly useful as a function of our own way of life if followed by conversation and catechizing, as was originally the case. However, you can and you will teach, that is, if your deeds help to give life to your judgement and your judgement life to your deeds.

355. There is no objection to the Three Unities when the subject is very simple; occasionally, however, three times three unities, happily intertwined, will produce a very pleasing effect.

356. When men drag women around with them, they will be spun off as though from a distaff.

357. It may happen that a man will be horribly thrashed by public and domestic disasters; but when callous fate comes in contact with rich sheaves, it simply crushes the straw; the grains, meanwhile, feel nothing, and leap around merrily on the barn floor, not caring whether they are on the way to the mill or to the field for sowing.

358. Arden of Feversham, Shakespeare's youthful work. It is altogether serious in its conception and execution, no trace of concern about its effect, perfectly dramatic, quite untheatrical.

359. Shakespeare's finest dramas occasionally lack ease: they are something more than they should be, and precisely on that account they point to the great poet.

360. The greatest probability of fulfilment still admits an element of doubt; that is why what you hope for is always surprising when it really happens.

361. You have to make allowances for all other arts; it is only Greek art that leaves you forever in its debt.

362. '*Vis superba formae.*' ['The superb strength of form.'] An attractive formulation by Johannes Secundus.

363. The sentimentality of the English is humorous and tender, that of the French is popular and tearful, of the Germans naïve and realistic.

364. The absurd, tastefully presented, arouses repugnance and admiration.

365. Of the best kind of society one used to say that its conversation is instructive, its silence formative.

366. Someone described a remarkable poem by one of the female sex as having more energy than enthusiasm, more character than content, more rhetoric than poetry, and, taking it all in all, there was something masculine about it.

367. There is nothing more dreadful than active ignorance.

368. You have to distance yourself from beauty and intelligence if you don't want to become their vassal.

369. Mysticism is the heart's scholastic learning, the dialectic of feeling.

370. One is indulgent towards old people as one is towards children.

371. An old person suffers the loss of one of the greatest human rights: he is no longer judged by his equals.

372. My experience with the natural sciences is like that of a man who gets up early and then in the dusky light of dawn impatiently awaits the early brightness of the sky, and yet is blinded when the sun actually appears.

373. There is, and there will continue to be, much argument about the usefulness and the damage of disseminating the Bible. It is clear to me that it will do damage, as hitherto, if it is used dogmatically and in a fantastic way: it will be useful, as heretofore, if it is accepted educationally and sensitively.

374. Great pristine forces, developed from all eternity or within time, work irresistibly, whether usefully or destructively is a matter of chance.

375. An 'idea' is something eternal and unique; it is not correct to use this term in the plural. Everything that enters our awareness and that we can talk about is no more than the manifestation of an 'idea'; we express concepts, and to that extent 'idea' is itself a concept.

376. In the context of aesthetics it is not apt to speak of 'the idea of beauty'; in this way you isolate the concept of beauty, which surely cannot be thought of as a separate entity. You can have a concept of what is beautiful and this concept can be transmitted.

377. The manifestation of the idea as beauty is just as fleeting as the manifestation of what is sublime, witty, amusing, ridiculous. This is what makes it so hard to talk about such topics.

378. It could be truly didactic if, in aesthetic matters, one were to take one's students past all that is worth registering with the senses or present it to them at its climax and when they are at their most receptive. But, as this demand cannot be fulfilled, the teacher lecturing from his desk should take his greatest pride into putting across the concepts of so many manifestations in such a way that the learners are made receptive to all that is good, beautiful, great, true, grasping it with joy when it comes upon them at the right moment. And then, without their noticing and knowing it, the basic idea from which it all proceeds would have become a living reality for them.

379. In considering educated people, one finds that they are receptive to only *one* manifestation of primordial being, in fact to only a few, and this is quite enough. The man of talent can work things out in practice and need not take notice of theoretical details: it will not disadvantage the musician to ignore the sculptor, and vice versa.

380. One should think of everything as it will work out in practice, and should therefore aim to achieve a fitting interaction of related aspects of the overall 'idea' in so far as these are to appear through people. Painting, sculpture and the miming arts are inseparably related; but the artist who feels called to one of these must beware of damaging effects from the other: the sculptor can allow himself to be seduced by the painter, the painter by the actor, and all three of them can confuse one another to such an extent that they can none of them stand on their feet.

381. Mimetic dance as an art form might really lead to the ruin of all the plastic arts, and rightly so. Fortunately the sensual attraction which this art form evokes is very fleeting and there has to be exaggeration if the attraction is to work. Fortunately this immediately frightens off other artists; but if they are wise and careful, they can learn a great deal in the process.

Vol. VI, issue 1: [untitled] (1827)

382. The first and last thing demanded of genius is love of truth.

383. He who is and remains true to himself and to others has the most attractive quality of the greatest talents.

Brocard

384. Art is the conveyor of the inexpressible; it therefore looks like folly again to attempt conveying it by words. But our effort to do this enriches our understanding in many ways, and this, in turn, is good for our potential.

Relationship, inclination, love, passion, habit

385. The kind of love whose violence youth feels is not fitting for old age, like everything that presupposes productivity. It is a rare thing for this to be maintained with the passing of years.

386. All real and all half-poets make us so familiar with love that it would have become trivial had it not constantly and by its very nature renewed itself in full power and splendour.

387. Quite apart from the way passion dominates and fetters a person, he is also tied up in many necessary relationships. Whoever is unaware of these or wants to transform them into love will inevitably become unhappy.

388. All love is connected with presence; what is agreeable to us by its presence always shows itself to us when it is absent and constantly makes us want its renewed presence, and, when this wish is granted, is accompanied by lively delight; when this joy persists we are filled by an ever-equal happiness – this is what we really love, and this means that we can love everything that can enter our presence; indeed, to formulate an ultimate statement: love of the divinity always strives to make what is highest present to us.

389. Inclination is closely related and not rarely develops into love. It is cognate to a pure relationship which resembles love in every way except that it does not necessarily demand continued presence.

390. This kind of inclination can point in many directions, be connected with many people and objects, can really make a person happy in a continuous process if he knows how to keep going. It is worth careful consideration that habit and custom can completely replace passionate love. What it demands is not just a charming presence, but a comfortable one; then, however, it is invincible. It takes a lot to break off a relationship to which one has become accustomed; it persists in spite of all that is objectionable; displeasure, vexation, anger, cannot prevail against it; indeed, it outlasts contempt, hatred. I don't know whether a novelist has ever managed a perfect description of it; he would, moreover, only have to try his hand at it casually, episodically; for if he tried to develop this theme more precisely, he would have to do battle with much that is improbable.

FROM THE *PERIODICAL ISSUES ON MORPHOLOGY*

Vol. I, issue 4: [untitled] (1822)

391. The supreme thing we have received from God and from nature is life, the rotating movement of the monad about itself, knowing neither rest nor repose; the instinct to foster and nurture life is indestructibly innate in everyone; its idiosyncrasy, however, remains a mystery to ourselves and to others.

392. The second favour bestowed by forces working on us from on high is the monad's inner experience, gradual apprehension of, then intervention in, the environments of the external world, the monad here being seen as a lively-mobile entity which, only by this process of intervention, actually becomes conscious of its own being as something unlimited within, but limited without. It is by this experience, though aptitude, attentiveness and luck also count, that we can reach clarity within ourselves; for some, however, this too must always remain a mystery.

393. As a third factor we develop what we reveal to the outside world by way of action and deed, of word and writing; this belongs to the world rather than to ourselves, and the world understands it more readily than we can; and yet the world feels that it needs to know as much as possible about our experience if it is to see quite clearly what we are doing. This is why people are most eager to read about youthful beginnings, stages of intellectual development, biographical incidents, anecdotes and things of that kind.

394. This outward effect is inevitably followed by a reaction, whether it is love seeking to further us or hatred knowing how to hold us back. The nature of this conflict varies little in the course of our life because man, too, remains like himself, this also being the case with everything that we in our own particular way like or dislike.

395. What friends do for us and with us is also a part of our living experience because it strengthens and furthers our personality. What enemies undertake against us is not part of our own living experience; it merely comes to our knowledge; we repudiate it and protect ourselves against it as we would against frost, storm, rain and hail, or other outer evils which are to be expected.

396. One is not inclined to live *with* just anyone, and, similarly, one can't live *for* everyone. Whoever really grasps this can greatly esteem his friends and not hate or persecute his enemies: there are, in fact, few things of greater advantage than learning to appreciate the good points of your opponents: this gives you decided superiority over them.

397. If we go back in history, we are always aware of personalities with whom we could get on and others with whom we should certainly be in conflict.

398. The most important thing is, however, our own contemporary time, because it is most clearly mirrored in us and we in it.

399. In his old age Cato was denounced in the law courts, and the chief point he made in his defence oration was that one couldn't plead one's case except before those with whom one had lived. And he is perfectly right: how is a jury to judge on premises which it simply has not got? How is it to take counsel about motives which are already far remote in time?

400. Experience is something we can all value, especially the man who is old and has time to think, to reflect; he has the confident, comfortable feeling that no one can rob him of this.

401. My nature studies, for instance, are based entirely on personal experience; who can take away from me the fact that I was born in 1749, and that (omitting a good deal) I faithfully toiled away at Erxleben's manual of *Naturestudy*, that I kept up with the subsequent editions inordinately piled up by the zeal of Lichtenberg; and that I didn't just read in print about new discoveries, but immediately came to know and inform myself about every new discovery as it was in progress, that I followed the great discoveries of the eighteenth century step by step right up to the present day, seeing them rise up before me like stars of wonder? Who can take away from me the secret joy of knowing that I myself, by unremitting attentive work, came so close to some great discovery which astonished the world? So close, in fact, that it seemed to break forth from my own innermost mind, as it were, and I then had a clear vision of the few steps which, in my darksome researches, I had failed to take?

402. Anyone who has witnessed the discovery of air balloons will testify to the world-wide movement this brought about, what concern surrounded the balloon navigators, what longing surged up in so many thousands of hearts to take part in such sky wanderings, long ago posited, prophesied, always believed in, always unbelievable; how fresh and circumstantial were the newspaper accounts of each single successful attempt, how there were special supplements and illustrated broadsheets, what tender concern there was for unfortunate victims of such attempts. It isn't possible to reconstruct this even in one's memory, just as one cannot recall the full vividness of our interest in a highly significant war which broke out thirty years ago.

403. The most attractive form of metempsychosis is when we see ourselves reappear in someone else.

404. Professor Zauper's *German Poetics* drawn from Goethe, as also the appendix to this study, Vienna 1822, do indeed make a gratifying impression on the poet; he feels as though he were walking past mirrors and sees himself portrayed in a favourable light.

405. And could this be any different? What our young friend experiences about us is of course action and deed, word and writing proceeding from us in happy moments which we are always glad to acknowledge as our own.

406. We very seldom satisfy ourselves; all the more consoling, therefore, to have satisfied others.

407. When we look back on our life we really only see it as something piecemeal, because our omissions and failures always surface first in our mind and dominate our actions and achievements.

408. Nothing of all this is apparent to the young man involved in the process; he sees, enjoys, makes use of the youth of a predecessor and in this way edifies himself from his own innermost being as though he had already at one time been what he now is.

409. In a similar, indeed identical, way, I rejoice in the manifold echoes reaching me from foreign lands. Foreign nations are later in getting to know our youthful works; their young men, their older men, striving and active, see their own image mirrored in us; they come to realize that we too wanted what they now want; they draw us into their companionship and give us the illusion of youth returning.

410. Scholarly knowledge is greatly retarded by our preoccupation with what is not worth knowing and with what is unknowable.

411. The higher form of empiricism relates to nature just as human reason relates to practical life.

412. When basic primitive phenomena appear unveiled to our perception, we feel a kind of timidity, even fear. Sense-bound people take refuge in astonishment; but along comes reason, that busy pander hurrying to mediate in its own way between the noblest and the most vulgar instincts.

413. Art is the true mediator. To speak about art is an attempt to mediate the mediator, but all the same this has brought us much delight.

414. Reasons for deduction are comparable to reasons for arrangement: both must be thought through completely, or else they are worthless.

415. Similarly in the sciences you really know nothing, you always have to do, to act.

416. Every true insight is part of a sequence and leads to a sequence. It is a link in a great chain mounting creatively.

417. Scientific knowledge helps us mainly because it makes the wonder to which we are called by nature rather more intelligible; and also in that it gives our ever-heightened life new skills to avert what is damaging and to introduce what is useful.

418. People complain that scientific academics do not intervene boldly enough in real life; that's not their fault, however, the reason being the whole approach to science and dealing with it.

FROM THE *PERIODICAL ISSUES ON THE NATURAL SCIENCES*

Vol. II, issue 1: *Old Ideas, Almost out of Date* (1823)

419. When a corpus of knowledge is ready to become a science, a crisis must necessarily arise; for a difference emerges between those who separate what is particular and give a separate account of it, and those who keep the general in view while wanting to add and integrate what is particular. Now as scientific, ideological and more comprehensive treatment enlists more and more friends, patrons and collaborators, this process of separation at a higher stage is perhaps less marked but still noticeable enough.

Those whom I would like to call the universalists are convinced and imagine that everything is always and everywhere there, even though in infinitely varied and manifold shape, and is also discoverable; others, whom I will term singularists, will concede the main point in general, indeed they observe, define and teach according to this principle, but they always want to find exceptions where type is not particularly marked, and here they are quite right. Their fault is just that they misunderstand basic form where it is overlaid and deny it altogether when it is hidden. As both these methods of apprehension are basic and will eternally remain in opposition without either uniting or cancelling one another out, one should beware of all controversy and make a clear and bare statement of one's convictions.

420. So I will repeat my own view: that at these higher stages one cannot know but must do, just as in a game there is little to know and everything to accomplish. Nature has given us the chessboard beyond which we cannot and would not wish to operate; nature has carved the counters whose value, moves and potentiality gradually become known to us: it is our part now to make moves which hold a promise of gain for us; everyone tries to do this in his own way and doesn't relish interference. So let this happen and make it our chief concern to observe carefully where we all stand, how close to or how distant from one another, and then harmonize to the best of our ability with those who own the belief which we ourselves profess. Let us, moreover, remember that we are always dealing with an insoluble problem, and should firmly and faithfully register whatever comes up for discussion, more especially whatever goes against the grain; for this is precisely where we first become aware of what is problematical, this residing, of course, in the actual object of inquiry but even in the human factor, in people. I am not quite sure whether I myself will go on experimenting in this well-worked field, but I do reserve my right to go on paying attention and drawing attention to this or that development of an inquiry, to this or that step taken by an individual.

421. Man cannot well go on existing on his own and this is why he likes to join a party, because this is where he finds, if not tranquillity, at least composure and security.

422. Maybe there are people who are by nature not up to this or that business; precipitation and prejudice are, however, dangerous demons, unfitting the most capable person, blocking all effectiveness and paralysing free progress. This applies to worldly affairs, particularly, too, to scholarship.

423. In the realm of nature, the dominant factors are motion and activity, in the realm of freedom it is predisposition and will. Motion is eternal and is irresistibly in evidence on every propitious occasion. Factors of predisposition also develop naturally, but must first be put into practice by the will and then heightened by degrees. That is why one cannot be as sure about the spontaneous will as about independent action: the latter operates of its own accord, the former is operated on. For the will, if it is to be made perfect and effective, must be subject, in the moral realm, to conscience that does not err, but in the realm of art it complies with a rule that is nowhere formulated. Conscience has no need of an antecedent as it is self-contained and only concerned with its own inner world. Genius might be in the same case of needing no rule, being self-sufficient, laying down its own rule; but as its field of action is the outside world, it is in many ways conditioned by its material and by time, with both of which there is bound to be difficulty. That is why everything connected with any art form, with its general management as with an individual poem, statue or painting, is so very curious and unpredictable.

424. It is a bad thing, happening, however, to quite a few observers, to make an immediate connection between an insight and a conclusion and to consider both as being equally valid.

425. The history of the sciences and of all that happens in their development shows us certain epochs which follow on, now in faster, now in slower sequence. A certain significant view, new or revived, is formulated; sooner or later it is recognized; it finds supporters, the result is passed on to students; it is taught and propagated and we note with regret that it doesn't matter whether or not this view is true or false; both take the same course, are finally formulated as a phrase; both are imprinted in the memory as a dead word.

426. Error is more particularly perpetuated by works which hand on the truth and error of the day in encyclopaedic form. Science cannot be expounded in this fashion where what is known, believed, surmised is included; this is why works of this kind look very odd after fifty years.

427. Begin by instructing yourself, then you will receive instruction from others.

428. Theories usually result from the precipitate reasoning of an impatient mind which would like to be rid of phenomena and replaces them with images, concepts, indeed often with mere words. One senses, possibly also realizes, that this is a mere makeshift; but doesn't passion and partiality always fall in love with makeshifts? And rightly so, because they are so greatly needed.

429. We attribute our circumstances now to God, now to the devil and are wrong in both cases: the conundrum lies in ourselves spawned as we are by two worlds. Colour is in the same case: now we look for it in light, now out in the cosmos, and we are unable to find it precisely where it is, in fact, at home.

430. A time will come when pathological experimental physics will be taught, and this will reveal in clear daylight all the sham argumentation which bypasses reason, surreptitiously wins conviction and, worst of all, completely prevents all practical progress. Phenomena must once and for all be removed from their gloomy empirical-mechanical-dogmatic torture chamber and submitted to the jury of plain common sense.

431. The fact that in his prismatic experiments Newton used the smallest possible opening, conveniently symbolizing a line to the ray of light, has brought incorrigible error into the world which will perhaps go on doing damage for centuries to come.

By this tiny hole Malus was led into wild theorizing, and had Seebeck been less circumspect, he would have been prevented from discovering the ultimate source of these phenomena, that is, entoptic figures and colours.

432. But what is really most extraordinary: even when a man has discovered the basic reason for the error, this does not mean that he has got rid of the error itself. A number of English scholars, especially Dr Reade, speak out passionately against Newton: the prismatic image, they say, is by no means the sun image, but that of the opening of our window shutters decorated with colour borders; that in the prismatic image there is no original green, this arises when blue and yellow merge so that a black line, just as a white one, could seem to be dissolved in colours, if one wants to use the term 'dissolve' in this instance. In short, all that we have been stating for years is now being similarly put forward by this good observer. But it so happens that the fixed idea of diverse refractability will not leave him, but he reverses it and is, if anything, even more caught up in this prejudice than his great master. Instead of being inspired by this new conviction and letting it release him from the chrysalis state, he tries to squeeze his grown and unfolded limbs back into the old husks of the pupa state.

433. Immediate perception of primeval phenomena makes us react with something akin to fear: we feel our inadequacy; it is only when they come alive through the eternal interplay of empiricism that we can react with joy.

434. The magnet is a primeval phenomenon where mere naming already serves as an explanation; that is how it becomes a symbol for all the rest for which we need not seek a name or words.

435. Everything that is alive surrounds itself with an atmosphere.

436. Exceptional men of the sixteenth and seventeenth century in themselves constituted an academy. When knowledge proliferated so tremendously, private individuals joined together so as to achieve as a body what was no longer within the capacity of a scholar working on his own. They kept well away from state ministers, princes and kings. How hard the hidden French scientific societies tried to do without Richelieu's help! How the English Oxford and London Society resisted the influence of Charles II and his favourites!

But once the change had actually come about, and the sciences looked on themselves as state members of the state body, and were granted their due rank in processions and other celebrations, their higher purpose was soon lost to view; men paraded their own person, and the sciences, too, were draped in their little gowns and had on their little bonnets. I have given extensive examples of this kind of thing in my *History of the Science of Colour*. But whatever has been recorded in writing has been written so that it may continually be made actual.

437. It is given to few to comprehend nature and put it to direct use; somewhere between their perception and its application people like to invent a gossamer airy fabric which they carefully extend, forgetting the object and at the same time its use.

438. Similarly, it is not easily understood that things happen in the great sphere of nature exactly as they do in the smallest compass. If experience forces it on people, they in the end put up with it. Straw, attracted by a rubbed piece of amber, is cognate to the most terrific thunderstorm, indeed, it is one and the same phenomenon. We concede this relationship between small and great in a few other cases, but the pure spirit of nature soon abandons us and the demon of artificial constructionism seizes hold of us and manages to assert its validity everywhere.

439. Nature has managed to keep enough freedom so as to prevent us from getting at it radically with our knowledge and science or actually cornering it.

440. It is hard to come to terms with the errors of the times: if you oppose them, you stand alone; if you allow yourself to be caught up in them, you get neither honour nor joy in the process.

FROM *WILHELM MEISTER'S JOURNEYMAN YEARS* (1829)

Thoughts about Art, Ethics and Nature in the Spirit of the Travellers

441. There's nothing clever that hasn't been thought of before – you've just got to try to think it all over again.

442. How can we learn self-knowledge? Never by taking thought but rather by action. Try to do your duty and you'll soon discover what you're like.

443. But what is your duty? The demands of the day.

444. The reasonable world is to be seen as a great individual not subject to mortality and forever bringing about what is needed, in this way even mastering chance events.

445. The longer I live, the more depressing I find the spectacle of a man, whose optimal function is to be a lord over nature so as to free himself and his fellow men from tyrannical necessity, doing the exact opposite of what he really wants to do, and all because of some preconceived false notion; and in the end, because the structure of the project as a whole has been ruined, he just muddles on miserably with odd details.

446. Man of ability and action, be worthy of, and expect:

grace	– from those who are great
favour	– from the powerful
a helping hand	– from those who are active and good
affection	– from the crowd
love	– from an individual

447. When a dilettante has done what lies within his capacity to complete a work, he usually makes the excuse that of course it's as yet unfinished. Clearly, it never can be finished because it was never properly started. The master of his art, by means of a few strokes, produces a finished work; fully worked out or not, it is already completed. The cleverest kind of dilettante gropes about in uncertainties and, as the work proceeds, the dubiousness of the initial structure becomes more and more apparent. Right at the end the faulty nature of the work, impossible to correct, shows up clearly and so, of course, the work can never be finished.

448. For true art there is no such thing as preparatory schooling, but there are certainly preparations; the best, however, is when the least pupil takes a share in the master's work. Colour-grinders have turned into very good artists.

449. Copycat work, casually stimulating people's natural activity in imitating an important artist who achieves with ease what is difficult, is quite a different matter.

450. We are quite convinced that it is essential for the artist to make studies from nature; we won't however deny that it often grieves us to perceive the misuse of such praiseworthy endeavours.

451. We are convinced that the young artist should rarely, if at all, set out to do studies from nature without at the same time considering how he might round off every sheet and make a whole of it, transforming this unit into a pleasing picture set within a frame, and offer it courteously to the amateur and the expert.

452. Much that is beautiful stands as an isolated entity in the world, but the spirit has to discover connections and thus to create works of art. The flower unfolds its full beauty only through the insect that clings to it, through the dewdrop that makes it glisten, through the calix from out of which it may be drawing its last sustenance. No bush, no tree whose charm may not be enhanced by a neighbouring rock or brook, by a simple prospect in the distance. And so it is with human figures and so with animals of every kind.

453. The advantages accruing to a young artist in this way are indeed manifold. He learns to think out the best way of fitting together related things and, when he thus composes intelligently, he will, in the end, assuredly not lack what is termed invention, the capacity to develop a manifold whole out of single units.

454. And, as well as conforming to the tenets of art pedagogy, he gains the great advantage, by no means to be despised, of learning to create saleable pictures that are a pleasure and delight to the art lover.

455. A work of this kind need not be complete down to the last detail; if it is well envisaged, thought out and finished, it is often more appealing to the art lover than a larger, more fully completed picture.

456. Let every young artist take a look at the studies in his sketch book and portfolio and consider how many of these sheets he might have been able to make enjoyable and desirable in this way.

457. We are not talking about the higher regions of art which might of course also be discussed; this is no more than a warning to recall the artist from a devious path and point the way to higher regions.

458. Let the artist put this to a practical test, if only for half a year, and not make use of either charcoal or brush unless he has the firm intention of actually structuring a picture out of the natural object or scene confronting him. If he has inborn talent, what we intended by our comments will soon be revealed.

459. Tell me with whom you consort and I will tell you who you are; if I know how you spend your time, then I know what might become of you.

460. Every individual must think in his own personal way; for on his way he always finds a truth or a kind of truth which helps him get through life. But he mustn't let himself go, he has got to keep a check on himself; purely naked instinct is unseemly.

461. Absolute activity, of whatever kind, ultimately leads to bankruptcy.

462. In the works of man as in those of nature, what most deserves notice is his intention.

463. People are at a loss with regard to themselves and one another because they use means as ends, and then, because of sheer busyness, nothing whatever happens or perhaps, even worse, something which is disagreeable.

464. What we think out, what we undertake, should have achieved such perfect clarity and beauty that anything the world could do to it could only spoil it; this would leave us with the advantage of only having to adjust what has been misplaced and refashion what has been destroyed.

465. Whole, half- and quarter-errors are most difficult and wearisome to put right, to sort out.

466. Truth need not always take corporeal form; enough for it to be around in spiritual form, bringing about harmony as it floats on the breeze as a spiritual presence like the solemn-friendly sound of bells.

467. When I ask young German artists, even those who have spent some time in Italy, why they use such crudely bright colours, especially in their landscapes, and seem to shun anything like harmony, they are apt to answer boldly and cheerfully that this is precisely how they see nature.

468. Kant has drawn our attention to the fact that there is such a thing as a Critique of Reason, and that this, the highest faculty possessed by man, has cause to keep watch over itself. Let everyone judge for himself what great advantages the voice of Kant has brought him. I, for my part, would similarly like to urge that a Critique of the Senses should be worked out, if art, especially German art, is in any way to recover and to proceed and progress at a pleasing and lively pace.

469. Man, born to be a creature of reason, nevertheless needs much education, whether this comes gradually by way of careful parents and tutors, by peaceful example or by stern experience. Similarly, there is such a thing as a born potential artist, but no one is born perfect. He may have an inborn clarity of vision, a happy eye for shape, proportion, movement: but without becoming aware of this lack, he may be without a natural instinct for composition in its higher aspects, for correct tonal proportion, for light, shade and colouring.

470. Now if he is not inclined to learn from more highly skilled contemporary or earlier artists what he himself lacks in order to be a true artist, he will lag behind his own potential because of a wrong-headed idea that he is safeguarding his own originality; for we own not just what we are born with, but also what we can acquire, and this is what we are.

471. General notions and great conceit are always potential creators of shocking misfortune.

472. 'You don't play the flute just by blowing – you've got to move your fingers.'

473. Botanists have a plant-category which they call 'Incompletae'; similarly one can say that there are incomplete and uncompleted people. These are the ones whose longings and strivings are out of proportion with what they actually do and what they achieve.

474. The least gifted man can be complete if he keeps within the limits of his capacities and skills, but real excellence is obscured, cancelled out and destroyed if there is not that absolutely essential sense of proportion. This disastrous lack is bound to crop up frequently in our own day; for who can possibly keep up with the demands of an exorbitant present, and that at maximum speed?

475. Only those people who are both clever and active, who are clear about their own capacities and can use them with moderation and common sense, will really get on in the world as it is.

476. A great failing: to see yourself as more than you are and to value yourself at less than your true worth.

477. From time to time I meet a young man whom I wouldn't wish different or improved in any way; but what worries me is that some of these people seem to me just the kind who let themselves drift along with the current of the stream of time, and this is where I keep wanting to point out that man is put at the helm of his own fragile craft precisely so that he may not follow the whim of the waves, the determination of his own insight.

478. But how is a young man independently to reach the insight that what everyone else pursues, approves and furthers may be reprehensible and damaging? Why shouldn't he let himself and his own natural disposition go the same way?

479. The greatest evil of our time – which lets nothing come to fruition – is, I think, that one moment consumes the next, wastes the day within that same day and so is always living from hand to mouth without achieving anything of substance. Don't we already have news-sheets for every point of the day! A clever man might well be able to slip in one or two more. In this way everything that anyone does, is working at or writing, indeed plans to write, is dragged out into the open. No one is allowed to be happy or miserable except as a pastime for the rest of the world, and so news rushes from house to house, from town to town, from one country to another, and, in the end, from one continent to the next, and all on the principle of speed and velocity.

480. As little as steam engines can be quelled, so little is this possible in the behavioural realm: the lively pace of trade, the rapid rush of paper-money, the inflated increase of debts made in order to pay off other debts, these are the monstrous elements to which a young man is now exposed. How good for him if nature has endowed him with a moderate and calm attitude so that he makes no disproportionate claims on the world nor yet allows it to determine his course!

481. But the spirit of the day threatens him in every sphere and nothing is more important than to make him realize early enough the direction in which his will should steer.

482. As one grows older, the most innocent talk and action grow in significance, and to those I see around me for any length of time I always try to point out the shades of difference between sincerity, frankness and indiscretion, and that there is really no difference between them, but just an intangible transition from the most harmless comment to the most damaging, and that this subtle transition has to be observed or indeed felt.

483. In this matter we have to use tact, else we run the risk of losing people's favour without being in the least aware of this and precisely in the way we came by it. This we probably come to understand in the course of life, but only after we have paid a high price for our experience, and from this we cannot, alas, spare those who come after us.

484. The relationship of the arts and the sciences to life is very varied according to the way their temporal stages are related to the nature of their epoch and a thousand other chance contingencies; which is why it isn't easy to make sense of all this.

Poetry is most effective at the start of any set of circumstances, irrespective of whether these are quite crude, half-cultured, or when a culture is in the process of change as it begins to become aware of a foreign culture; in such cases one can claim the effect of the new is definitely to be felt.

485. Music at its best hardly needs to be new; indeed, the older it is, the more familiar to us, the more effective it can be.

486. The dignity of art perhaps appears most eminent in music because it has no material of a kind for which detailed accounting might be needed. It is all form and content and it heightens and ennobles all it expresses.

487. Music is either sacred or profane. What is sacred accords completely with its nobility, and this is where music most immediately influences life; such influence remains unchanged at all times and in every epoch. Profane music should be altogether cheerful.

488. Music of a kind that mixes the sacred with the profane is godless and shoddy music which goes in for expressing feeble, wretched, deplorable feelings, and is just insipid. For it is not serious enough to be sacred and it lacks the chief quality of the opposite kind: cheerfulness.

489. The numinous nature of church music, the cheerfulness and playfulness of folk melodies are the two pivots of true music. At these two focal points music always and inevitably leads either towards reverence or else to dance. Any mixture of the two is confusing, dilution is boring, and if music consorts with didactic or descriptive poems and texts of that kind, the result is coldness.

490. Plastic art is really only effective at its highest level; it is true that the middle zone can perhaps impress us for more reasons than one, but all middle-range art of this kind is more confusing than gladdening. Sculpture therefore has to discover subject-matter of interest and this is to be found in the portraits of people of some significance. But here, too, it has to reach a high degree of excellence if it is to be at the same time true and dignified.

491. Painting is the slackest and most easy-going of all the arts. The slackest because, on account of the material and subject-matter, we condone and enjoy much that is no more than skilled craftsmanship and can hardly be called art. In part it is also because a good technical performance, even though it may be dull, can be admired by the cultured as well as the uneducated, and need only remotely resemble art in order to be highly acceptable. True colours, surfaces and a true relationship of visible objects – all this is in itself pleasing; and, since the eye is in any case used to seeing everything, it does not find misshapen or mistaken form as objectionable as a jarring note is for the listening ear. We tolerate the worst portrayal because we are used to seeing even worse originals. So the painter need only be remotely artistic so as to find a bigger public than a musician of equal merit; the minor painter can at least always operate on his own, whereas the minor musician has to associate with others in order to achieve some sort of resonance by means of a combined musical effort.

492. The question 'Are we to compare or not to compare when considering works of art' is one we would like to answer as follows: the trained connoisseur should make comparisons, for he has a general idea, a preconceived notion of what could be and should be achieved; the amateur, still involved in the process of being educated, can make the best progress if he does not compare but judges each achievement on its individual merit: this gradually forms an instinct and idea for the general situation. Comparison by the unknowing is really only a lazy and conceited way of avoiding judgement.

493. To find and to appreciate goodness everywhere is the sign of a love of truth.

494. The sign of a historical feeling for humanity is that, at the same time as we appreciate the merits and attainments of the present, we also take into account the merits of the past.

495. The best we get from history is that it rouses our enthusiasm.

496. Idiosyncrasy calls forth idiosyncrasy.

497. One has to remember that there are quite a lot of people who would like to say something significant without being productive, and then the most peculiar things see the light of day.

498. People who think deeply and seriously are on bad terms with the public.

499. If I'm to listen to someone else's opinion, it must be put in a positive way; I have enough problematic speculations in my own head.

500. Superstition is innate in the human make-up, and when you think you have completely ousted it, it takes refuge in the strangest nooks and crannies and then suddenly emerges when one thinks one is tolerably safe.

501. We would know much more about things if we weren't intent on discerning them too precisely. For, surely, an object can only be comprehensible to us when viewed at an angle of forty-five degrees.

502. Microscopes and telescopes really only serve to confuse the unaided human senses.

503. I hold my peace about many things; for I don't like to confuse people and am quite content if they are happy while I am cross.

504. Everything that liberates our mind without at the same time imparting self-control is pernicious.

505. The 'what' of a work of art interests people more than the 'how'; they can grasp the subject-matter in detail but not the method as a whole. That is why they pick out individual passages, in which, if you observe closely, the total effect is not actually lost but remains unconscious to all.

506. And the question, too, 'Where has the poet got it from?' gets no further than the 'what'; it helps no one to understand the 'how'.

507. Imagination is only ordered and structured by poetry. There is nothing more awful than imagination devoid of taste.

508. Mannerism is an ideology gone wrong, a subjective ideology; that's why, as a rule, it isn't without wit.

509. The philologist is dependent on the congruence of what has been handed down in written form. There is a basic manuscript and this has real gaps, errors of transcription which lead to a break in the meaning and to other difficulties common to manuscript tradition. Then a second copy is found, a third one; collating these leads to growing perception of what makes sense and meaning in the transmitted material. Indeed, the philologist goes further and requires that it should increasingly reveal and structure its inner meaning and the congruence of its subject-matter without dependence on philological aides. This calls for a special degree of sensitive judgement, a special absorption in an author long dead and a certain amount of inventive power; one cannot, therefore, take it amiss if the philologist allows himself to make a judgement in matters of taste even if this doesn't always succeed.

510. The poet is dependent on representation, the climax of which is reached when it vies with reality, that is, when the descriptions are so full of living power that everyone can see them as being actually present. At the summit of its excellence poetry appears as something completely external; the more it withdraws into the inner realm, the more it is on its way towards sinking. The kind of poetry which concentrates on the inner realm without giving it outward substance or without allowing the outward to be perceived through the inward – both are the last steps from which poetry steps down into ordinary life.

511. Oratory is dependent on all the advantages of poetry, on all its rights. It takes possession of these and misuses them in order to get hold of certain outer momentary advantages, whether moral or immoral, in civic life.

512. Literature is the fragment of fragments; only the least amount of what has happened and has been spoken was written down, the least of what has been recorded in writing has survived.

513. Although Lord Byron's talent is wild and uncomfortable in its structure, hardly anyone can compare with him in natural truth and grandeur.

514. The really important value of folksong, so called, is that its themes are taken directly from nature. But the educated poet too might well avail himself of this advantage if only he knew how to set about it.

515. But the advantage inherent in folksong is that natural people, as distinct from the educated, are on better terms with what is laconic.

516. Shakespeare is dangerous reading for talents in the process of formation: he forces them to reproduce him, and they imagine they are producing themselves.

517. Nobody can make judgements about history except those who have experienced history as a part of their own development. This applies to whole nations. The Germans have only been able to judge literature since the point they themselves have had literature.

518. One is really only alive when one enjoys the good will of others.

519. Piety is not an end but a means to attain by the greatest peace of mind the highest degree of culture.

520. This is why we may say that those who parade piety as a purpose and an aim mostly turn into hypocrites.

521. 'When one is old one has to do more than when one was young.'

522. A duty absolved still feels like an unpaid debt, because one can never quite live up to one's expectations.

523. Human failings are only descried by an unloving person; that is why, in order to realize them, one has to become unloving oneself, but not more than is strictly to the purpose.

524. It is our greatest good fortune to have our failings corrected and our faults adjusted.

525. If you can read, you should understand; if you can write, you have to know something; if you can believe, you ought to comprehend; if you desire, you will feel an obligation; if you demand, you will not get what you want; and if you are experienced, you ought to make yourself useful.

526. We only recognize the authority of those who are useful to us. We acknowledge the duke because we see our property secure under his aegis. We expect his protection in the face of external and internal contingencies that are untoward.

527. The brook is the miller's friend, useful to him and happy to rush over his wheels; no point, surely, in slow, indifferent progress along the valley.

528. One who is content just to experience life and act accordingly has all the truth he needs. This is the wisdom of the growing child.

529. Theory pure and simple is no use except in that it makes us believe in the interconnection of phenomena.

530. By application everything abstract is brought within the capacity of human reason, and this is how action and observation lead human reason to the power of abstraction.

531. He who demands too much, who rejoices in what is complex, is exposed to the danger of aberrations.

532. We mustn't scorn thinking that proceeds by way of analogies: analogy has the advantage of not closing doors or in fact aiming at any ultimate solution; the kind of inductive thinking, on the other hand, which has a preconceived purpose in view and is working towards it is damaging in that it sweeps both falsehood and truth along with it.

533. *Ordinary* viewing, a right conception of earthly matters, is the heritage of general human reason; *pure* viewing of what is external and internal is very rare.

534. The former finds expression in practical ways, in immediate action; the latter is symbolical and expressed chiefly in mathematics, numbers and formulas, in discourse, as something wholly original, in tropes, as the poetry of genius, as proverbial utterance of human reason.

535. What is remote from us influences us by means of transmission. In its usual form it may be described as historical; a higher form is related to the imagination, is mythical. If we look behind this form for a third factor, for some further meaning, it is transformed into mysticism. Moreover, it easily becomes sentimental so that we can only assimilate what we find congenial.

536. Ways of effective progress to be looked out for if we really want to get on are those of a kind that

> prepare,
> accompany,
> reinforce,
> help along,
> further,
> strengthen,
> hinder,
> confirm.

537. In meditation as in action we must make a distinction between what is accessible and what is inaccessible; failing this, little can be accomplished either in life or in knowledge.

538. '*Le sens commun est le génie de l'humanité.*' ['Common sense is the genius of humanity.']

539. Common sense, which is said to be the genius of mankind, must first of all be considered in the ways it finds expression. If we consider how mankind uses it, we find the following:

Mankind is conditioned by needs; if these are not satisfied, there is impatience; if they are, there is indifference. Human kind therefore moves between these two states and will use his understanding to satisfy needs; when this is done his task is to replenish the voids of indifference. If this remains within the most proximate limits, he manages this successfully. But if needs arise and go beyond the ordinary sphere, plain common sense is no longer adequate, it no longer acts as a 'genius'; the region of error opens up before mankind.

540. Nothing unreasonable happens, nothing that understanding or chance cannot put right again; nothing reasonable that a lack of understanding, or else chance, cannot lead astray.

541. Every great idea, as soon as it makes its appearance, has a tyrannical effect, and that is why the advantages it brings are all too soon transformed into disadvantages. One can therefore defend and praise every institution by pointing back to its beginnings and explaining that everything valid at the beginning is still valid now.

542. Lessing, a man who was unwillingly hemmed in by all kinds of limitations, lets one of his characters say: 'There's no need for anyone to "have to".' A witty man said: 'He who wills, has to.' A third one, admittedly an educated man, added: 'He who understands also wills.' And so people assumed that the whole sphere of understanding, willing and having to, had been settled for good. But, on the whole, a person's understanding, of whatever kind it may be, also determines what he does and what he does not do; which is why nothing is more frightful than to see ignorance in action.

543. There are two peaceful powers: law and decency.

544. Law deals with guilt, the police with what is fitting. Law considers and decides, the police surveys and commands. Law is concerned with the individual, the police with the community.

545. The history of learning is a great fugue in the course of which the voices of nations gradually emerge.

546. There are some problems in the natural sciences which cannot be adequately discussed without involving the help of metaphysics; not just, however, a school and word-wisdom, but the kind that existed before, with and after physics, that now is and will be hereafter.

547. Authoritative confirmation that something has in fact already happened, been said or decided in the past, is of great value; but only the pedant insists on authority at every juncture.

548. We honour an old basic foundation, but must not relinquish our right to structure a completely new one elsewhere at some other time.

549. Stand firm where you are – a maxim which is all the more necessary

than ever now that people are impelled to form great parties while, in another way, each individual is doing his utmost to put himself across according to his own point of view.

550. It is always better for us to say straight out what we think without wanting to prove much; for all the proofs we put forward are really just variations on our own opinions, and people who are otherwise minded listen neither to one nor to the other.

551. As I grow in knowledge of the natural sciences and become increasingly familiar and attached to them in their day by day progress, I am often struck by the fact that both their progressive and regressive movement take place simultaneously. May I just add one point for now: that we do not manage to get rid of even admitted errors in science. The reason for this is an open secret.

552. I call it an error when some event or other is wrongly analysed, wrongly associated, wrongly deduced. It may, however, happen in the course of new experience and thinking that a phenomenon is consequentially associated, rightly deduced. We're happy to accept that, but without specially valuing it, being quite content to allow the error to persist alongside; and I know of a little store-house full of errors kept in careful custody.

553. As people are, after all, not really interested in anything but their own opinion, everybody who formulates an opinion looks right and left for ways and means to support his own morale and that of others. We make use of truth as long as it serves a purpose; what is false, however, is seized upon with emotional rhetoric as soon as it can for the moment serve as a partial but dazzling argument, as a stop-gap which can apparently confer unity on the bits and pieces. Discovering this was annoying to begin with, then I was grieved about it and now I feel a kind of malicious joy: I have promised myself never again to reveal a procedure of this kind.

554. Everything that exists is an analogue of all existing things; that is

why existence always and at the same time looks to us both separate and interlocked. If you pursue this analogy too closely, everything coincides identically; if you avoid it, all is scattered into infinity. In both cases contemplation stagnates, either as hyperactive, or else as done to death.

555. Reason is dependent on what is coming into being, understanding depends on what is already there; the former is unconcerned about 'what for?', the latter doesn't ask 'where from?' Reason rejoices in the process of development; understanding wants to keep hold of everything so as to put it to use.

556. It is characteristic of man, an innate quality closely textured into the fabric of his being, that what is closest to him does not suffice for cognition. This is because every phenomenon which we ourselves observe is for that moment whatever is closest to us, and we can expect it to be self-explanatory if we tackle it with determination.

557. But people will not learn this as it goes against their nature; and that is why even educated people, when they recognize some truth or other in a precise place, cannot resist linking it not just with what is close by, but also with what is furthest away and most remote, a process leading to error upon error. But there is only one way a phenomenon nearby is related to a distant one, namely, that everything relates to a few great laws which are everywhere made manifest.

558.   What is general?
                                The individual case.
                                What is specific?
                                Millions of cases.

559. Analogy must guard against two deviations: firstly indulging in wit, which dissolves it altogether; or else donning a cloak of metaphor and image, which, however, does less damage.

560. Scholarship must not tolerate either mythology or legends. Leave these to the poets whose vocation it is to put them to use for the world's profit and joy. The scholarly man limits himself to the nearest, clearest present time. If, however, he has an occasional urge to be rhetorical, let him not be denied this indulgence.

561. In order to save my reason, I view all phenomena as independent units and try to isolate each from the other by sheer force; then I view them as correlatives and they combine to form vital structures. I apply this in the first instance to nature; but it can also be a way of looking at things which proves fruitful when applied to the latest turbulence of world history all around us.

562. Everything we call invention, discovery in a higher sense, is the significant practice, activation of an original instinct for truth, long developed in secret, which suddenly and at lightning speed turns into a fruitful perception. Developing from within, it is an outward manifestation which affords man a presentiment of his likeness to God. It is a synthesis of world and spirit conferring the most blissful assurance of the eternal harmony of existence.

563. Man must persist in the belief that the incomprehensible is, in fact, comprehensible; else he would cease to do research.

564. Each specific fact which can be made use of in any way is understandable. In this way what is incomprehensible can become useful.

565. There is a delicate form of empiricism which enters into the closest union with its object and is therefore transformed into an actual theory. But this heightening of spiritual capacity belongs to a highly civilized epoch.

566. Censorious observers and capricious theorists are the most revolting of all; their experiments are petty and complicated, their hypotheses abstruse and odd.

567. There are pedants who are at the same time rascals and these are the worst of all.

568. You don't have to travel all round the world in order to understand that the sky is blue everywhere.

569. The general and the particular coincide; the particular is the general made manifest under different conditions.

570. You don't have to have seen or experienced everything for yourself; but if you want to trust another person and his descriptions, remember that you are now dealing with three factors: with the matter itself and two subjects.

571. Fundamental characteristic of the living unit: to separate, to reunite, to expand into generality, to remain individual, to transform and to specify itself; and because what is alive can be made manifest in a thousand conditions, it can come to the fore and disappear, solidify and melt away, grow rigid and flow freely, expand and contract. And because all these effects happen at the same moment of time, each and every event can occur simultaneously. Appearance and disappearance, creation and destruction, birth and death, joy and sorrow, all is effective through and together with everything else, in the same sense and in the same measure; and this is why even the most specific thing that occurs is always revealed as an image and a parallel of what is most general.

572. As the whole of existence is an eternal process of separation and union, it also follows that human beings, watching and considering this tremendous process, will be now separating, now uniting.

573. Physics and mathematics must present themselves as distinct and separate from one another. The former must maintain decisive independence and attempt with all loving, respectful, devout endeavour to penetrate fully into nature and its sacred life, quite unconcerned with what mathematics, for its part, is achieving and doing. The latter, on the other hand, must declare itself independent of all outer things, follow its own great intellectual way and develop itself more perfectly than is possible if, as heretofore, it continues to deal with what is on hand, trying to extract something from it or make some adaptation.

574. Scientific research needs a categorical imperative just as it is needed in the sphere of morality; but we must remember that this doesn't bring us to a conclusion but only to a beginning.

575. Everything factual is already theory: to understand this would be the greatest possible achievement. The blueness of the sky reveals the basic law of chromatics. Don't go looking for anything beyond phenomena: they are themselves what they teach, the doctrine.

576. There is much certainty in the sciences provided we don't allow ourselves to be misled by exceptions and know how to honour problems.

577. If the primordial phenomenon finally reassures me, it is but resignation in another form; however, it is very different if resignation comes at the frontier of human thinking or within the hypothetical confines of my own narrow individuality.

578. When one looks at Aristotle's problems, one is astonished by his gift to notice and observe, and by the host of things for which the Greeks had an eye. But they commit the great fault of precipitation because they immediately pass from the phenomenon to its explanation, which leads to quite inadequate theoretical pronouncements. This, however, is the common fault, still committed nowadays.

579. Hypotheses are the cradle songs with which a teacher rocks his pupils to sleep; a faithful observer who reflects to some purpose is always more and more aware of his limitations and realizes that the wider the extent of his knowledge, the more problems make their appearance.

580. Our fault is that we cast doubt on what is certain and would like to pin down what is uncertain. My maxim in my research about nature is: keep hold of what is certain and watch out for what is uncertain.

581. I call it an excusable hypothesis when we are, as it were, positing it for fun so as to invite refutation from nature in earnest.

582. How could a man claim to be a master of his subject if he taught nothing that's unnecessary!

583. The craziest thing is that everyone imagines he has got to pass on what people have imagined they knew.

584. A didactic lecture is expected to provide certainty as the learner doesn't want to acquire doubtful information; this means that the teacher may not abandon any problem or possibly circumvent it at a distance. There must be immediate, fixed certainty ('*bepaalt*' [marked with pales] as the Dutchman puts it); then one imagines for a while that the unknown space is a sure possession, until someone else uproots the pales and then immediately sets them up again, fixing them closer together or else further apart.

585. Lively questioning about cause, confusing cause and effect, reposing in a wrong theory – all this does great, irreparable damage.

586. If some people hadn't felt obliged to repeat what is untrue simply because they had at one point maintained it, they would have turned into quite different people.

587. What is false has the advantage that it can always be the subject of gossipy chat; what is true has to be put to immediate use, else it isn't there.

588. He who fails to understand what a boon truth in the practical sphere can be subjects it to critical fuss and bother so as somewhat to embellish his own wrong-headed, laborious procedures.

589. The Germans, and they are not alone in this, have the gift of making the sciences inaccessible.

590. The English are masters at putting discovery to immediate use so that it leads to new discovery and fresh achievement. Now ask why they are everywhere ahead of us.

591. A man who thinks indulges a curious habit of replacing an unsolved problem with a fantasy he can't get rid of even after the problem has been solved and truth made evident.

592. It takes a special turn of mind to grasp formless reality in its essential nature and to distinguish it from the figments of the imagination which, all the same, thrust themselves urgently on our attention with a certain semblance of reality.

593. When contemplating nature, whether in great things or small, I have constantly asked the question: is it the object which is here declaring itself, or is it you yourself? And this is also my stance to predecessors and fellow workers.

594. Each and every person really looks on the world in its finished, regulated, formed, perfect aspect as no more than an element out of which he is trying to create a special world, one suited to his own measure. Competent people seize on the world without hesitation and seek to act as things come; others hang back, some even doubt its existence.

Anyone really penetrated by this basic truth would seek no quarrel with anyone else, but would only consider another man's view, as also his own, to be no more than just a phenomenon. For it is an almost daily experience that someone can think with ease along lines impossible for another person; and this not only in matters having any influence for weal or woe, but in matters which are of complete indifference to us.

595. We know what we know really only for ourselves. If I talk to someone else about what I believe I know, he forthwith imagines he knows it a lot better, and over and over again I have to turn back into myself with my knowledge.

596. Truth is constructive; error is unproductive, it only constrains us.

597. Man finds himself in the midst of effects and cannot resist inquiring into causes; taking the line of least resistance, he fixes on the nearest as the best, and this pacifies him; for this is more particularly the way of human reason.

598. When you see some evil you proceed to immediate action, you make an immediate attack to cure the symptom.

599. Reason is exclusively concerned with what is alive; the already created world, which is the concern of geognosy, is dead. This is why there can be no such thing as geology, because there is nothing here for reason to do.

600. If I find a scattered skeleton, I can gather up and structure the pieces; for eternal reason speaks to me here by an analogy, be it even that of the ground sloth.

601. We cannot envisage as coming into being what is no longer involved in this process; what has already come into being is beyond our understanding.

602. Vulcanism in its general new form is really a bold attempt to make a connection between the present incomprehensible world and an unknown world that has vanished.

603. The forces of nature produce the same or at least similar effects in different ways.

604. Nothing is more disagreeable than a majority; for it consists of a few powerful people in the lead, rogues who are adaptable, weak people who assimilate with the rest, and the crowd that trundles along behind without the slightest notion of what it's after.

605. Mathematics, like dialectics, is an organ of the inner higher intelligence; in practice it is an art, like oratory. Nothing is of value to them both except form: content is a matter of indifference. Mathematics may be calculating pennies or guineas, rhetoric defending truth or falsehood, it's all the same to both of them.

606. But here all depends on the nature of the person engaged in such an occupation, practising an art of this kind. A really incisive lawyer defending a just cause, a thoroughly perceptive mathematician contemplating the star-filled sky are both god-like.

607. What is exact about mathematics except exactitude? And this, is it not the result of an innate sense of truth?

608. Mathematics cannot remove prejudice, is unable to appease party bias, has no power in the whole moral domain.

609. A mathematician is only perfect in so far as he is a perfect man, sensitive to the beauty of truth; only on this condition will he make the impression of someone thorough, transparent, circumspect, clean, clear, attractive, indeed elegant. It takes all this to make him resemble Lagrange.

610. It is not language in itself that is correct, effective, graceful; it is the spirit embodied within language; so it is not a matter of an individual's power of choice whether he wants to imbue his calculations, his speeches or poems with desirable qualities: the question is: has nature blessed him with the intellectual and ethical qualities working towards this end? In the intellect: the capacity to contemplate and perceive; in the ethical realm: the power to repudiate the wicked demons who can frustrate his efforts to give the place of honour to truth.

611. The desire to explain what is simple by what is complex, what is easy by what is difficult, is a calamity affecting the whole body of science, known, it is true, to men of insight, but not generally admitted.

612. An exact inspection of physics will show that the phenomena, as also the experiments, on which it is built up vary in value.

613. Everything depends on the primary original experiments, and the chapter built up on this basis stands safe and firm. But there are also secondary experiments, tertiary ones and so on; concede them equal authority, and they only confuse what was made clear by the first.

614. It does great damage to the sciences, indeed, everywhere, that people who have no capacity for abstract thinking make bold to theorize, not grasping the fact that however much knowledge they have, this does not entitle them to theorize. Initially they may well set to work with laudable common sense, but this has its limits; transgress them, and even common sense runs the risk of becoming absurd. The territory and inherited portion assigned to it is the area of doing and acting. Common sense engaged in activity will rarely go astray; more complex thinking, inference and judgement are not, however, its business.

615. To begin with, experience is of use to science, then it does damage because experience leads to an awareness of law and exception. Drawing the average between them by no means results in truth.

616. Truth, so it is said, is situated at the central point between two opposing views. Not at all! The problem itself lies between the two, that which is beyond our range of vision, eternally active life, contemplated in repose.

From Makarie's Archive

617. One cannot and may not reveal secrets about the way people lead their lives; there are stumbling blocks of a kind to trip up every traveller. The poet, however, points to the significant place along the road.

618. It wouldn't be worthwhile reaching the age of seventy if the sum total of the world's wisdom were folly before God.

619. Truth is god-like: it is not immediately perceptible; we are obliged to guess it from its manifestations.

620. The true pupil learns how to develop the unknown from the known and gets close to his master.

621. But people lack the capacity to develop the unknown from the known; for they don't know that their reason plays similar tricks on them as nature herself.

622. For the gods teach us to imitate their very own work; but we only know what we ourselves are doing, without, however, realizing what it is we are imitating.

623. All is like, all unlike; all is useful and harmful, eloquent and dumb, reasonable and unreasonable. And what people profess about individual matters is often contradictory.

624. For law has been laid down by mankind on itself without knowledge of the subject of legislation; but nature was set in order by all the gods.

625. What man has laid down just doesn't fit, be it right or wrong; but what the gods lay down is always in place, right or wrong.

626. I, however, want to show that the known arts of man are like natural occurrences which proceed openly or in secret.

627. Prophecy is an art of this kind. It describes what is hidden within what is apparent, the future within the present, life within what is dead and the sense of what is senseless.

628. So the instructed man always rightly understands man's nature, the uninstructed sees it now in one way, now in another, and everyone mimes it in his own way.

629. When the union between a man and a woman leads to a boy child, an unknown entity results from something known. When, on the other hand, the boy's dark spirit absorbs clearly distinct things, he grows into a man and learns to recognize the future from out of what is here and now present.

630. What is immortal is not comparable with what is mortal yet alive; but what is merely alive is capable of understanding. Thus the stomach knows very well when it is hungry and thirsty.

631. This is the respective roles of the art of divination and of human nature. And the man of understanding can come to right terms with either, while the man of limited vision sees them now in one way now in another.

632. At the blacksmith's forge iron is made malleable by using bellows on the fire and removing superfluous nourishment from the iron stave; but once that stave has been cleared it is beaten and forced, and, nourished by water coming from outside, it regains its strength. This is what happens to man through the agency of his teacher.

633. 'As we are convinced that he who surveys the world of the intellect and apprehends the beauty of its author's intellect may well also take due note of its father who is exalted above all understanding, we therefore try to involve all our faculties in the attempt to realize and to express on our own account – in so far as such matters can be clarified – how we may contemplate the beauty of its spirit and of the cosmos.'

634. 'So let us assume that two blocks of stone are placed side by side, the one left in its crude state without artistic fashioning, the other formed by art into a statue of a god or a man. If godly, it might represent one of the graces or the muses; if human, it need not be a specific person, but rather a creation in which art has concentrated all beauty.'

635. 'But to you the stone which art has fashioned into beautiful form will immediately appear as something beautiful; not, however, as stone

– else the other block would also be seen as beautiful – but because of the form given to it by art.'

636. 'The material, however, did not have a form like this, but this was present earlier in the man's thinking before it got as far as the stone. Yet it was in the artist not because he had eyes and hands but because he was endowed with the gift of art.'

637. 'And this means that even greater beauty exists in art itself, because it is not the form latent in art which comes across into the stone; the form stays there and another lesser and derived beauty emerges which does not remain a self-contained entity, nor yet as the artist would have wished it to be, but exists only to the extent to which the material has complied with the art that fashioned it.'

638. 'If, however, art actually manages to create that which it is and what it contains, and makes visible a beauty in harmony with reason according to which it always operates, it is indeed art of greater and more excellent beauty, more perfect than anything that appears externally.'

639. 'And so, in that form, becoming apparent by entering into a material already diffused outwardly, it is weaker than that which is concentrated in a single entity. For what is distanced from itself is dispersed from its own self: strength leaves strength, warmth leaves warmth, power leaves power, and so, too, beauty leaves beauty. Hence that which is at work must be more excellent than that which has been worked. For it is not "un-music" but music that makes the musician, and music which is beyond the senses brings forth music accessible to the senses.'

640. 'But if anyone were to despise the arts because they imitate nature, one can only reply that natural objects are themselves imitation, and, furthermore, that the arts do not precisely imitate what the eye sees, but go back to that fundamental principle of reason which constitutes nature and according to which it acts.'

641. 'Furthermore, the arts bring forth much out of themselves and, on the other hand, add some features lacking to perfection as they contain beauty within themselves. Thus Phidias was able to create the form of a god, even though he was not imitating any model visible to the senses, but was conceiving a god in his own imagination – as Zeus himself might appear if he became visible to our eyes.'

642. You cannot blame idealists of ancient and modern times for so vigorously urging people to mark well the one single unity from which all things spring and to which everything is, it seems, to return. For, of course, the vivifying and ordering principle is so straitened in its manifestation that it scarcely knows how to save itself. On the other hand, however, we also go short if we force back the forming principle and the higher form itself into a single unity which is in the course of vanishing before our outer and inner apprehension.

643. We human beings are entirely dependent on extension and movement; it is in these two general forms that all other forms, especially those perceptible to the senses, are made manifest. A spiritual form, however, is in no way lessened when it is made outwardly apparent, provided that its emergence is a true generation, a truly new birth. What is generated is not less good than its generator; indeed, it is the advantage of living generation that the end-product can be more excellent than what generates it.

644. It would be of real importance to develop and illustrate this matter in an essentially practical way. But a circumstantial, logically sequent exposition might well make excessive demands on the listeners' attention.

645. You can't get rid of what really belongs to you, even if you throw it away.

646. The latest philosophy of our western neighbours is a witness to the fact that, however he acts, a man, and even whole nations, will always revert to their own innate tendencies. And how could this be otherwise, as this determines his nature and his whole way of life?

86

647. The French have renounced materialism and have conceded rather more spirit and life to primitive beginnings; they have freed themselves from sensualism and have allowed the depths of human nature some kind of intrinsic development; they allow for the validity of productive power and do not try to explain all art by the imitation of externally perceived objects. May they persevere in such directions.

648. There can be no such thing as an eclectic philosophy, but there can be eclectic philosophers.

649. But an eclectic is everyone who, from whatever exists and is happening around him, makes his own the things he finds congenial to his nature; and this context validly includes all that can be called culture and progress in a theoretical and practical sense.

650. It follows that two eclectic philosophers could turn into the greatest opponents if they are antagonistic to one another, and each, for his part, picks out whatever is congenial to him in every traditional system of philosophy. Just look round and you'll find that this is the way every man always acts and so can't imagine why he is unable to convert others to his own way of thinking.

651. If you look more closely, you find that even the historian does not easily see history as historical; for each writer of history always writes as if he had himself been there at the time, and not about what actually was in the past and moved people. Even the writer of a chronicle points more or less to the limitations, the characteristics of his town, his monastery or his age.

652. It is rare even for a man of the greatest age to come to see himself as historical, or for his contemporaries to be seen as historical by him; the result is that there is no one left with whom he is either inclined or able to enter into argument.

653. Various proverbs of the Ancients which one is in the habit of repeating to oneself had a completely different significance from that which later ages would like to give them.

654. The saying that no one unacquainted with geometry, a stranger to geometry, should enter the Philosophers' school does not, of course, mean that one must be a mathematician in order to be a sage.

655. Geometry is here understood in its initial elements as we have it in Euclid and as we let every beginner start it. It is, moreover, the most perfect preparation, indeed introduction, to philosophy.

656. When the boy begins to grasp that a visible point must be preceded by an invisible one, that the shortest way between two points is already thought of as a line before the pencil draws it on the paper, he feels a certain pride and pleasure. And quite rightly; for the source of all thinking has been opened up to him, idea and realization, '*potentia et actu*', has become clear to him; the philosopher has nothing new to tell him, the basis of all thinking has dawned on the geometer within his own sphere.

657. If we take the significant dictum 'Know yourself', and consider it, we mustn't interpret it from an ascetical standpoint. It does not by any means signify the kind of self-knowledge advocated by our modern hypochondriacs, humorists and '*Heautontimorumens*' [self-torturers], but quite simply means: pay some attention to yourself, watch what you are doing so that you come to realize how you stand *vis-à-vis* your fellows and the world in general. This needs no psychological self-torture; any capable person knows and appreciates this. It is good advice and of the greatest practical advantage to everyone.

658. The great thing about the Ancients, especially the Socratic school, is that they set before us the sources and guidelines of all life and action, not for the purpose of idle speculation, but as a call to life and deeds.

659. If our teaching in schools always continues to point to Antiquity and promotes the teaching of the Greek and Latin languages, we can congratulate ourselves that these studies, so essential for any higher culture, will never suffer decline.

660. For if we look upon Antiquity with the firm intention of educating ourselves, we are rewarded by the feeling that this is really the beginning of our true humanity.

661. The Schoolman trying his hand at writing and speaking Latin sees himself as more elevated and distinguished than he is allowed to be in his everyday life.

662. In the face of Antiquity any mind sensitive to poetical and artistic creation feels transported to the most delightful and ideal state of nature; and, right up to the present day, the songs of Homer have the power to deliver us, if only for brief moments, from the fearsome load with which tradition has weighed us down over many thousands of years.

663. As Socrates made an appeal to moral man so that he might quite simply become somewhat clearer about himself, so too Plato and Aristotle looked on nature as competent individuals: the former seeking to adapt himself by spirit and temperament, the latter to win it by analytical insight and method. And so every approach we can make to these three philosophers, as a whole or in detail, is an event that fills us with the greatest joy and always furthers our education in the most positive way.

664. If we are to rescue ourselves from the boundless multiplicity, atomization and complexity of the modern natural sciences and get back to the realm of simplicity, we must always consider the question: how would Plato have reacted to nature, fundamentally one unity as it still is, how would he have viewed what may now appear to us as its greater complexity?

665. For we think we can definitely assume that we can attain to the final ramifications of cognition in the same organic way, and that from this position we can gradually build up and consolidate the summit of every kind of knowledge. However, we shall have to examine day by day how the spirit of the age we live in either furthers or obstructs our effort, if we are not to dismiss what is useful and absorb what is harmful to our endeavours.

666. The eighteenth century is praised for mainly concentrating on analysis; this leaves for the nineteenth century the task of discovering the false syntheses still obtaining and of making a renewed analysis of their content.

667. There are only two true religions: one where the numinous in and all around us is acknowledged and worshipped without any form, the other where the form is of the greatest beauty. Everything intermediate is idolatry.

668. It cannot be denied that the Reformation was an attempt by the spirit to free itself; enlightenment about Greek and Roman Antiquity brought a longing for a freer, more decent and becoming kind of life. This desire was heightened by the heart's longing to return to a certain simple state of nature and by the imagination's quest for a concentrated focus.

669. All the saints were suddenly banished from heaven, and man's senses, thoughts and feelings were directed away from a heavenly mother and her tender child towards a grown man intent on moral action and suffering unjustly; he was then transfigured as a demi-god and later acknowledged and venerated as true God.

670. His background was the creator's whole extended universe; spiritual influence emanated from him, his suffering was seized upon as a model and his transfiguration as the pledge of everlasting life.

671. Just as incense refreshes the life of an ember, so prayer refreshes the hopes of the heart.

672. I am convinced that the Bible becomes more and more beautiful the more one understands it, that is, the more one realizes and sees that every word which we take as being of general application and as special for ourselves had an individual, particular and immediate relevance according to certain conditions and circumstances of time and place.

673. If we look closely, we still have to reform ourselves every day and protest against others, even if not in a religious sense.

674. We have the inescapable, utterly serious intention, renewable day by day, to grasp and understand the word as a most immediate meeting point with what we feel, see, think, experience, imagine and consider reasonable.

675. Let everyone examine himself and he will find this much more difficult than one might think; for unfortunately people see words as surrogates: they think and know better than what they actually manage to put into words.

676. But let us try to eliminate as far as possible what might insinuate itself as false, inappropriate, inadequate in ourselves and in others, and let us do this by steady endeavour, clarity and uprightness.

677. Advancing years bring greater trials.

678. When I have to cease being moral, I am left without power.

679. Censorship and freedom of the press will always be at loggerheads. The man of power demands and imposes censorship, the lesser man asks for freedom of the press. In his plans and activities, the former does not want to be hindered by clamorous contradictory attitudes, but, rather, obeyed; while the latter wants to voice his reasons so as to legitimize his disobedience. This, you will find, is the universal rule.

680. But it should also be noted here that the weaker and suffering man, in his own way, also tries to suppress freedom of the press, namely when he is himself engaged in conspiracy and wants to avoid being betrayed.

681. One is never deceived, one deceives oneself.

682. We need a word in our language which, in the way that 'childhood' relates to child, expresses the relationship of the concept 'peoplehood' to 'people'. The tutor must listen to and hear 'childhood', not 'the child'; the legislator and regent must hear 'peoplehood', not 'the people'. The former always voices the same thing, is reasonable, consistent, clear and true; the latter, because of much wanting, never knows what it wants. And in this sense law can be and should be the voice of the will of 'peoplehood'. A will never formulated by the crowd, but heard by the understanding listener, satisfied by one who is reasonable and gladly appeased by the good ruler.

683. We don't ask by what right we rule: we simply rule. We are not concerned whether people have any right to depose us: we just take care that they are not tempted to do it.

684. We wouldn't object if death could be abolished; but abolishing the death penalty will be difficult to put across. If it is abolished, we shall occasionally reinstate it.

685. If society gives up the right to make use of the death penalty, self-help immediately takes over: vendetta knocks at the door.

686. All laws are made by the old and by men. Young people and womenfolk want the exception, the old want the rule.

687. It is not the discerning man who governs, but discernment; not the reasonable man, but reason.

688. When you praise someone, you are putting yourself on a par with him.

689. Knowledge is not enough, we have to apply it; wanting is not enough, there has to be action.

690. There is no such thing as patriotic art and patriotic scholarship. Both these, like everything great and good, belong to the whole world and can be developed only by a general free interaction on the part of all our contemporaries and with constant reference to the past and to what is known about it.

691. Scholarly knowledge tends, on the whole, to be remote from life and only returns to it via a detour.

692. For the sciences are really compendia of life: they connect and establish outer and inner experiences in an interrelated context.

693. Basically the sciences are only of interest in a specialized world, that of scholarship; for involving the rest of the world and informing it in this field, as has happened in more recent times, is an abuse and does more harm than good.

694. The sciences should only affect the world by means of higher practical application; for they are really all of them esoteric and can only become exoteric if they correct some form of activity. All other participation leads nowhere.

695. The sciences, considered within their own inner circle, are in fact treated with immediate interest, every time. A powerful stimulus, particularly by something new and unheard of, or at least by something greatly advanced, arouses general attention which can go on for years and which has proved to be particularly fruitful in the recent past.

696. A significant fact, an ingenious *aperçu*, occupies a very great number of people, first as they get to know about it, then as they come to understand it, work on it and extend its scope.

697. About any new important matter the crowd always asks what use it is, nor is this unwarranted; for it is only by its usefulness that the crowd can come to understand the value of anything.

698. True sages ask what a matter is in itself and in relation to other matters, and they are unconcerned about its usefulness, that is, the way it can be applied to what is familiar and necessary for life; for all that kind of thing will, in due course, be discovered by minds of quite different cast, by sharp-witted people who revel in life, have technical expertise and are versatile.

699. Spurious sages only try to draw some personal profit, and that as quickly as possible, from any new discovery; they are out for empty renown as they attempt, now to develop, now to increase, now to improve, to stake a rapid claim or perhaps even take advance possession of a discovery. By such immature procedures they make true science unsafe and confuse it, and indeed they stunt its most excellent result, namely its practical flowering.

700. The most damaging prejudice is the idea that any kind of research into nature might be laid under an interdict.

701. Every research worker must see himself exactly as though he were someone called to serve on a jury. All he has to do is to make sure that his exposition is complete and is explained by clear evidence. On this basis he summarizes his conviction and casts his vote, whether or not his opinion coincides with that of the man who will report on it.

702. He then remains equally calm when the majority is on his side as when he finds himself in a minority; for he has done his part: he has expressed his conviction, he is not lord over minds and attitudes.

703. Scholars of this kind, however, have never wanted to count as important in the world of scholarship: in general, people are out to rule and dominate, and because very few are really independent, the crowd draws the individual along in its wake.

704. The history of philosophy, of the sciences, of religion, all show that opinions are spread abroad on a quantitative scale and that the leading position always goes to what is easier to grasp, that is, to whatever is easier and more comfortable for the human spirit. Indeed, the man who has fully educated and developed himself in a higher sense can always reckon to have the majority against him.

705. If nature in its lifeless beginning were not so thoroughly stereometric, how would it, in the end, attain unaccountable and immeasurable life?

706. Man in himself, in so far as he is using his sound senses, is the greatest and most exact 'physical', i.e. scientific apparatus that can be imagined, and this, precisely, is the most disastrous aspect of modern physics: that experiments have been, as it were, segregated from the human factor and that nature is to be recognized only by the evidence of artificial instruments and in this way limits what nature wants to achieve and prove.

707. Similarly in the matter of calculation. Much that cannot be calculated is true just as in the case of a great deal that cannot be taken as far as a decisive experiment.

708. But that is precisely why man stands so high – that what is otherwise not representable can be represented in him. For what is a string in a musical instrument and all its mechanical grades compared with the musician's ear! Indeed, one can say: what are the elemental phenomena of nature itself compared with man, who has first of all to tame and modify them so as to assimilate them in some small degree to his own purposes!

709. Too much is demanded of an experiment if it is to achieve everything within its own compass. Thus, to begin with, electricity could only be demonstrated by the action of rubbing, whereas now its most impressive aspect is produced merely by contact.

710. Just as one will never be able to dispute the leading position and effectiveness of the French language as a highly developed court- and world-language with the potential of continuous further development, so too it will never occur to anyone to underestimate the debt which the world owed to mathematicians who deal with the most important matters in their own language; for they have the capacity to regulate, determine and decide everything that is subject in the highest sense to number and to measurement.

711. Every thinking man who looks at his calendar, his watch, will remember to whom he owes these benefits. But even if we acknowledge and concede such benefits in time and space with due reverence, we will realize that we are all, in fact, in touch with what goes far beyond these spheres, with something that belongs to us all and without which nothing could either be done or achieved: idea and love.

712. 'Who knows anything about electricity,' said a joking scientist, 'except when he strokes a cat in the dark or when lightning and thunder flash and roar down around him? How much and how little does he know about it then?'

713. We can use Lichtenberg's writings like a marvellous magic wand: wherever he cracks a joke, a problem lies hidden.

714. He also had a cheerful idea about the void and vacant area of the universe between Mars and Jupiter. When Kant had carefully proved that these two planets had consumed and appropriated all the available matter to be found in this void area, Lichtenberg said in his flippant way: 'Why shouldn't there be such things as invisible worlds?' And wasn't he perfectly right? Are not the newly discovered planets invisible to the whole world, except for the few astronomers to whose word and calculation we have to give credence?

715. Nothing is more damaging to a new truth than an old error.

716. People are so harassed by the infinitely conditional nature of phenomena that they fail to perceive the one basic phenomenon.

717. 'When travellers revel very joyfully in mountain climbing, I feel that this is something barbaric, even godless. Mountains do of course give us an idea of the power of nature, not, however, of a kindly providence. Of what practical use are they to human beings? If a man decides to live way up in the mountains, his house will be buried or shifted by an avalanche in the winter and by a landslide in the summer; the mountain torrent drowns and carries off his flocks, storms sweep away his storage barns full of wheat. When he sets out on his way, every ascent is the torture of Sisyphus, every descent the fall of Vulcan; day by day his path is littered with stones and disappears, the mountain torrent is impossible to navigate. Even if his stunted animals find precarious nourishment, or he provides them with a miserable supply of fodder, the elements, or else wild beasts, carry off his herds. He leads a solitary wretched life like the moss growing on a tombstone, devoid of comfort and company. And these zigzag crests, these hateful rock-faces, these deformed pyramids which cover the most beautiful stretches of the world with all the horror of the North Pole – how can a kind-hearted man possibly take pleasure in them and any friend of man sing their praises?'

718. As an answer to this worthy man's paradoxical utterances one might reply that if God and nature had willed to develop and continue the primal mountain complex from Nubia right through to the west and as far as the great ocean, and, furthermore, to sever this mountain range a few times in a north–south direction, this would have created valleys where many a Father Abraham and many an Albert Julius, a 'Felsenburg', would have found a land of Canaan where his descendants, easily rivalling the stars in number, could have increased and multiplied.

719. Stones are silent teachers, they make those who study them dumb, and the best to be learnt from them is incommunicable.

720. What I really know, I know only for myself; an uttered word is seldom of constructive value: it mostly leads to contradiction, hesitation and to a standstill.

721. Seen as a science, crystallography is an altogether unusual case. It is not productive, it is just itself, not giving rise to anything else, more especially now that a number of isomorphic bodies have been found which turn out to be quite distinct according their content. As it really is not possible to apply crystallography in any way, it has developed largely as something self-contained. It gives the mind a certain limited satisfaction and is so manifold in its detail that it can be called inexhaustible; which is the reason why it keeps a lasting and decisive hold on outstanding people.

722. Crystallography has something of the monk and the confirmed bachelor about it, and it is therefore sufficient unto itself. It has no practical influence in a living context; for its most precious products, crystalline gems, first have to be cut and polished before we can use them to adorn our womenfolk.

723. The opposite can be said of chemistry, which can be applied in the most extensive way and proves to be of the most unlimited influence on life.

724. The concept of coming into being is completely denied to us, which is why, when we watch something coming into being, we imagine that it has always been there. That is why we can grasp the system of encapsulation, of things being contained one within another.

725. How much that is significant we see as constituted of various parts: look at architectural works; one sees a great deal piled up in regular and irregular ways. That is why the atomistic concept is close by and readily at hand for us; and why we are not afraid of applying it also in organic cases.

726. Anyone unable to grasp the difference between a fantasy and an idea, between the realm of law and that of hypothesis, is in a bad way as a scientist.

727. There are hypotheses where intelligence and imagination replace the idea.

728. It doesn't do to dally too long in the realm of the abstract – what is esoteric is damaging when it strives to be exoteric. Life is best taught by what is alive.

729. The kind of woman who can replace her children's father, should he not be there, is considered the most excellent.

730. The invaluable advantage accruing to foreigners who only now come to a thorough study of our literature is that they are immediately raised high above the early illnesses of its development which we ourselves have had to suffer in the course of the century; and if luck holds, they can in this way enjoy most desirable instruction.

731. Where the eighteenth-century French are destructive, Wieland teases.

732. Poetical talent is given to the peasant just as to the knight; what matters is that each should make the best of his condition and treat it with dignity.

733. 'What are tragedies but versified passions of people who make goodness knows what of external circumstances?'

734. In future it will not be possible to use the word 'school' in the context of the German theatre as one would use it in the history of art and in speaking, for instance, of a Florentine, Roman and Venetian school. It is a term which one might still have used some thirty or forty years ago when training of a natural artistic kind in more limited circumstances could still be envisaged; for, to speak more precisely, the word 'school' in connection with the arts is really only right for the initial stages, for as soon as it has produced outstanding artists its influence is immediately extended abroad. Florence shows its influence on France and Spain; the Netherlands and Germany learn from Italy and gain more liberty of mind and spirit, while, in exchange, southerners learn a happier technique and the most precise execution from the north.

735. The German theatre has now reached the stage of finality, general education being so widespread that it cannot continue to belong to a single locality or proceed from one particular point.

736. The basis of all theatrical art, as of any other form of art, is truth and what accords with nature. The more weighty such art is, the higher the level at which the poet and the actors manage to grasp it, the higher will be the standing of the stage. Germany enjoys great advantage in this respect because reciting good poetry has become a more general practice and has also spread beyond the theatre.

737. The basis of all recitation is declamation and mime. As the actual recitation is the only thing that matters and has to be practised in reading aloud, it is obvious that this kind of reading remains the school of truth and naturalness if men undertaking such work are convinced of the value, the dignity of their profession.

738. Shakespeare and Calderón have provided a splendid entry into this kind of reading aloud; however, one ought to consider whether the impressive strangeness, this talent soaring to a point of unreality, may not be precisely what could prove damaging to German training in this respect.

739. Individuality of expression is the beginning and end of all art. But every nation has a particular quality distinct from the individuality of mankind in general; this may repel us to begin with, but if we were to put up with it, to yield ourselves up to its influence, it could, in the end, overpower and stifle our own individual nature.

740. How much that is false have Shakespeare, and, more particularly, Calderón, brought upon us, how these two great lights in the poetical heavens have turned into misleading lights, into a will-o'-the-wisp — let this be decided by future literary historians.

741. Nowhere can I condone that we should put ourselves completely on a par with the Spanish theatre. Calderón, this splendid dramatist, has so much that is conventional that an impartial observer is hard put to recognize his poetical talents hidden beneath all the etiquette of theatre. And if one confronts any audience with this kind of thing, one always takes its good will for granted, assuming that it will agree to accept something completely alien to its own world if it is to take pleasure in a foreign meaning, tone and rhythm, abandoning for a time what is really its own true bent.

742. Yorick-Sterne's spirit was the most attractive ever; reading him invariably makes one feel free and good; his type of humour is inimitable, and not every kind of humour can set the soul free.

743. 'Moderation and a clear sky are Apollo and the Muses.'

744. 'Sight is the noblest sense. The other four only inform us via our organs of tactile apprehension: we hear, feel, smell, touch by contact; sight, however, is of infinitely higher standing, rises more subtly above what is material and gets close to spiritual faculties.'

745. 'If we put ourselves in the place of other people, the jealousy and hatred we so often feel about them would disappear, and if we put others in our place, pride and conceit would greatly diminish.'

746. 'Someone compared reflection and action with Rachel and Leah: one was more attractive, the other more fruitful.'

747. 'Nothing in the world except health and virtue is more to be treasured than knowledge and learning; nor is anything so easily attainable and so cheap to acquire: all you have to do is to be still, all you have to spend is time, something we cannot save in any other way than by spending it.'

748. 'If one could store time as one can store ready money without using it, half the world would take this as an excuse for laziness, though only up to a point; for this would be like a household where one lives on capital without bothering about the interest.'

749. 'Modern poets put a lot of water into their ink.'

750. 'Among the many curious stupidities of the schools, none seems to me so ridiculous as the strife about the authenticity of old writings, old works. For I ask you, is it the author or the works we are admiring or censuring? Our sole concern is always and only the author before us; why should we bother about the names when we are interpreting a work of the spirit?'

751. 'Who can maintain that it is Virgil or Homer we have before us when we are reading the works ascribed to them? But our business is with the writers, and what more do we want? And, indeed, it seems to me that the scholars who are so pernickety about this unimportant matter are no wiser than a very pretty woman who once asked me, with the sweetest possible smile, who was, in fact, the author of Shakespeare's plays.'

752. 'It is better to do the most unimportant thing in the world than to look on half an hour as unimportant.'

753. 'Courage and modesty are the least ambiguous virtues; for they are of a kind that hypocrisy cannot mime. They also have in common the fact that they find expression in a similar colouring.'

754. 'In the thieving fraternity fools are the worst: they filch both your time and your temper.'

755. 'Respecting ourselves determines our morals; valuing others rules our behaviour.'

756. 'Art and learning are words so often used and whose precise difference is so rarely understood, the one is often used for the other.'

757. 'Nor do I like the definitions given of them. Somewhere I once found a comparison between learning and wit, art and humour. This seems to me to be imagination rather than philosophy: maybe it gives us some idea of the difference between the two but not of the particular qualities of each.'

758. 'I think one could describe learning as knowledge of things in general, extracted knowledge; art, on the other hand, would be learning used for action. Learning would be reason, and art its mechanism; in the end, learning would be the theorem, art the problem.'

759. 'Perhaps one might make the following objection: poetry is deemed an art and yet it is not mechanical. But I deny that it is an art; nor yet is it learning. The arts and systems of learning are acquired by thinking, not so poetry; for this is inspiration: it was conceived in the soul when it first stirred into life. We ought to call it neither an art, nor learning, but genius.'

760. And now, too, at this present moment, every educated man should have another look at Sterne's works so that the nineteenth century, too, should discover what we owe him and realize what we might go on owing him in future.

761. Literary success tends to obscure what was influential at an earlier time, covering up what has resulted from this earlier work; that is why it is advisable to look back from time to time. Whatever is original about us is best preserved and commended when we don't lose sight of our forefathers.

762. May the study of Greek and Roman literature ever remain the basis of higher education!

763. Chinese, Indian, Egyptian antiquities are never more than curiosities; it is a very good thing to acquaint oneself and the world with them; but they will bear but little fruit for our moral and aesthetic education.

764. There is no greater danger for the German than to extol himself as compared with his neighbour and by means of him. No nation, perhaps, is more suited to developing out of its own self, which is why it was of the greatest possible advantage that the outside world was so late in paying it any attention.

765. If we see that our literature lags behind for over half a century, we find that nothing was done with foreigners in mind.

766. But that Frederick the Great didn't want to know anything at all about them did, however, irritate the Germans and they did their best to appear to some advantage in his eyes.

767. Now that the concept of world literature is on the way in, the German, if you look closely, has most to lose: he will do well to think carefully about this warning.

768. Even people of sensitive understanding fail to realize that they are trying to explain basic experiences the thought of which ought, in fact, to reassure and calm us.

769. However, this may be all to the good, else research would be abandoned too soon.

770. From now on, anyone who doesn't take up some art or some manual trade will be in a bad way. Learning fails to bring advancement now that the world is caught up in such a rapid turnover; by the time you have managed to take due note of everything you have lost your own self.

771. The world in any case forces general education on us, so we don't really trouble to acquire it; special knowledge depends on our own efforts.

772. The greatest difficulties are situated where we're not looking for them.

773. Laurence Sterne was born in 1713 and died in 1768. In order to understand him one must not lose sight of the moral and ecclesiastical culture of his time; and remember in this connection that he was Warburton's contemporary.

774. A free soul like his runs the danger of rudeness unless noble benevolence establishes moral balance.

775. His reactions were very sensitive while at the same time they all developed from within himself; by a process of continual conflict he distinguished truth from falsehood, clung to the former and was intransigent against the latter.

776. He felt definite hatred for solemnity because it is didactic and dogmatic and quite easily turns pedantic, a quality for which he nursed the most definite loathing. Hence his dislike of terminology.

777. In his wide-ranging reading he spotted inadequacy and ridiculousness everywhere.

778. He defines Shandeism as the spirit which will not suffer him to think for as long as two moments upon any grave subject.

779. This rapid alternation between gravity and jesting, caring and indifference, grief and joy, is said to be inherent in the Irish character.

780. His sagacity and penetration are boundless.

781. His cheerfulness, his frugality and long-suffering while on his travels, where these qualities are put to a severe test, do not find their equal anywhere.

782. However greatly the sight of a free soul of this kind amuses us, we are also reminded, in this very case, that we may not assimilate all this, or at least most of it, for our own selves.

783. The element of lasciviousness which he handles with such delicate skill and intelligence would be the downfall of many others.

784. His attitude to his wife as to the world in general is worth noting: 'I have not made use of my misery like a wise man,' he says somewhere.

785. He jokes most charmingly about the contradictions which make his condition ambiguous.

786. 'I cannot bear preaching; I fancy I got a surfeit of it in my younger days.'

787. In no respect is he a model, in every way he suggests and stimulates.

788. 'Our concern about public affairs is mostly just philistinism.'

789. 'Nothing should be treasured more highly than the value of the day.'

790. '*Pereant qui ante nos nostra dixerunt!*' ['May they perish, all those who said before us what we are saying now!']
   Only someone who imagined himself to be an original could possibly say this kind of thing. Anyone who prides himself on being descended from reasonable ancestors will surely attribute just as much common sense to them as he does to himself.

791. The most original authors of the day are not rated as such because they produce something new, but only because they are capable of saying this kind of thing as though it had never been said before.

792. That is why the most attractive mark of originality is knowing how to develop a received idea so creatively that no one can easily guess how much lies hidden within it.

793. Many ideas appear only quite gradually like flowers opening out among the greenery of the branches. When roses are in season, one sees roses in bloom everywhere.

794. In the end all depends on attitudes: where there are mental attitudes, ideas follow, and ideas are in keeping with attitudes.

795. 'Nothing is reproduced quite impartially. One might say that the mirror is an exception here, and yet we never see our face quite rightly in reflection; indeed, the mirror reverses our figure and makes our left hand into our right. This can be taken as a model image of all our reflections about ourselves.'

796. 'In the spring and autumn one doesn't easily think about a fire on the hearth, and yet if we happen to see one in passing, we find the feeling it gives us so pleasant that we want to linger. This might be seen as analogous to any temptation.'

797. 'Don't be impatient if your arguments are not accepted as valid.'

798. Anyone who lives for a long time in important circumstances does not, of course, encounter everything that it is possible for a person to experience; yet he will experience what is analogous to this, and perhaps also some things that are without precedent.

POSTHUMOUS

On Literature and Life

799. Every great idea which comes into the world as a gospel turns into an offence for hesitant and pedantic people, and into a folly for those of wide but shallow culture.

800. Each and every idea makes its appearance like an unknown guest, and as it begins to enter the sphere of reality is hardly distinguishable from what is imaginary and fantastic.

801. This is what has been termed 'ideology' in the good and also in the bad sense, and why the ideologist is so greatly disliked by everyday people who are actively practical.

802. Every direct call to idealism is a serious matter, especially for the female of the species. Inevitably, an outstanding man on his own finds himself at the centre of a more or less religio-moralistic-aesthetic seraglio.

803. All empiricists are on the search for ideas and cannot discover them in multiplicity; all theorists are looking for them in multiplicity and fail to discover them there.

804. But both types find their way to one another in life, in action, in art, and this is so often repeated; few, however, understand how to make use of this.

805. One can recognize the usefulness of an idea and yet fail to understand just how to make the best use of it.

806. Every stage of life corresponds to a certain philosophy. A child appears as a realist; for it is as certain of the existence of pears and apples as it is of its own being. A young man, caught up in the storm of his inner passions, has to pay attention to himself, look and feel ahead; he is transformed into an idealist. A grown man, on the other hand, has every reason to be a sceptic; he is well advised to doubt whether the means he has chosen to achieve his purpose can really be right. Before action and in the course of action he has every reason to keep his mind flexible so that he will not have to grieve later on about a wrong choice. An old man, however, will always avow mysticism. He sees that so much seems to depend on chance: unreason succeeds, reason fails, fortune and misfortune unexpectedly come to the same thing in the end; this is how things are, how they were, and old age comes to rest in him who is, who was and ever will be.

807. Researching into nature we are pantheists, writing poetry we are polytheists, morally we are monotheists.

808. Critical reason has done away with the teleological proof of the existence of God; we put up with this. But what cannot be proved should remain valid to us as feeling, and we go back to all these pious notions from Brontotheology to Niphotheology. Should we not be allowed to feel in lightning, thunder and storm the closeness of a more than mighty power, in the scent of blossoms and the gentle stirring of a warm breeze a being that comes lovingly close to us?

809. 'I believe in one God!' This is a fine and praiseworthy dictum; but to recognize and proclaim God wherever and however he may reveal himself, that is actually bliss here on earth.

810. If you want to deny that nature is a divine organ, you might as well deny all revelation.

811. 'Nature hides God!' But not from everyone!

812. Kepler said: 'My supreme desire is to be aware inwardly, as it were in my inner self, of the God I find everywhere outside myself.' This noble man, not consciously realizing it, was in fact at that very moment feeling the most exact fusion between the divine in himself and the divine in the universe.

813. If our standing is high, God is all; if low, then God is a supplement to our wretchedness.

814. A creature is very weak; for when it seeks it does not find. But God is strong; for if he is looking for a creature he immediately has it in his hand.

815. Faith is love for what is invisible, trust in what is impossible, improbable.

816. Mythology = *Luxe de croyance.*

817. What is *Praedestinatio*? Answer: God is more powerful and wiser than we are; therefore he deals with us as he pleases.

818. Christianity contrasts far more strongly with Jewish belief than with paganism.

819. The Christian religion was intended to be a political revolution which, when it failed, became a moral one later on.

820. There are theologians who wish there had been only one single person in the world whom God had redeemed; for then there could not have been any heretics.

821. 'The Church weakens everything that it touches.'

822. Apocrypha: it would be important to make a new summary of all that is historically known on this subject and to show that it is precisely this corpus of apocryphal writings that flooded even the congregations of the first centuries and from which our canon still suffers; this is, too, the real reason why Christianity could never at any given moment of its political and ecclesiastical history appear in all its beauty and purity.

823. Aural confession at its best is a continued catechism for adults.

824. In New York, it is said, there are now ninety Christian churches of divergent confessions, and this town is now amassing inordinate wealth, especially since the opening of the Erie Canal. Probably people are of the opinion that religious thoughts and feelings, of whatever specific kind, belong to the pacifying atmosphere of Sunday, while strenuous activity, accompanied by pious sentiments, belongs to the workaday world.

825. If a good word finds a good home, as the saying goes, then a pious word finds an even better one.

826. It is all-important in missionary work that crude, sensual man should realize that there is such a thing as morality, that a passionate, uncontrolled man should understand that he has been guilty of transgressions for which he cannot forgive himself. The former leads to the adoption of sensitive maxims, the latter to belief in reconciliation. All middling, apparently casual faults will be committed to the care of an all-wise, unfathomable guidance.

827. Where lamps burn you have oil stains; where candles burn there's snuff; only the heavenly lights shine clear and without blemish.

828. 'Perfection is the norm of heaven, perfect performance is humanity's required norm.'

829. Duty: where one loves what one orders oneself to do.

830. A right-minded man always considers himself to be more distinguished and more powerful than he actually is.

831. All laws are attempts to approach the intentions of the moral world-order in the course of the world and of life.

832. It is better for you to experience injustice than for the world to be without law. Therefore everyone should subscribe to law.

833. It is better that there should be acts of injustice than that they should be unjustly remedied.

834. During the four years of the interregnum – which is what I call the rule of Galba, Otho, Vitellius – Nero would have been incapable of creating disaster of the kind that befell the world after he was murdered.

835. If God had intended people to live and act in truth, then he would have had to arrange things differently.

836. One could say, by way of a joke, that man is composed entirely of faults, some of which are found to be useful to society, others damaging, some of service, others of none. One speaks well of the former: calls them virtues; ill of the latter: calls them faults.

837. Man is not only what he was born with, but what he has attained.

838. It is our qualities we should cultivate, not our idiosyncrasies.

839. Character in important and less important matters is that a man should steadily pursue whatever course he feels to be within his capacity.

840. It is soon evident where there is a lack of the two most necessary qualities: spiritual power and authority.

841. Our opinions are only supplementary to our existence. A person's way of thinking shows what he lacks. The emptiest people think very highly of themselves, the first-rate are mistrustful, a vicious person is impertinent and a good man is anxious. So everything is set in balance; everybody wants to be whole or to appear whole in his own eyes.

842. Considered historically, our good points appear in a moderate light, our faults excuse themselves.

843. He who doesn't see his lover's faults as virtues is not in love.

844. You can't love anyone unless you can be sure of his presence when you need him.

845. You only know those who cause you suffering.

846. You only keep a watch on those who cause you suffering. If you want to remain unknown to the world, all that's needed is not to hurt anyone.

847. There is a great difference between living in someone and living with someone. There are people in whom one can live without living with them, and vice versa. To combine both is only possible where there is absolute love and friendship.

848. It is better to be deceived in one's friends rather than deceiving one's friends.

849. When two people are really happy about one another, one can generally assume that they are mistaken.

850. A wolf in sheep's clothing is less dangerous than a sheep in any sort of clothing, which would make one take it for a mere wether.

851. Don't say that you want to give, but go ahead and *give*! You'll never catch up with a mere hope.

852. One would give generous alms if one had eyes to see the beauty of a cupped receiving hand.

853. To do well you need talent, to do good you need means.

854. If you have dropped a quill pen, you should pick it up at once, else it will be trodden underfoot and destroyed.

855. There is no art in turning a goddess into a witch, a virgin into a whore, but the opposite operation, to give dignity to what has been scorned, to make the degraded desirable, that calls either for art or for character.

856. There is no situation which cannot be ennobled by work or else by endurance.

857. You forgive everything to someone who is in despair; you give the poverty-stricken every chance to earn something.

858. In some quiet hour when they were sociably together, Faith, Love and Hope felt an urge to fashion something new; they set to work together and created a lovable new quality, a higher kind of Pandora: Patience.

859. Lasciviousness: playing with what is to be enjoyed, playing after it has been enjoyed.

860. Vanity is craving for personal renown: it is not for your qualities, merits, actions you want to be esteemed, honoured, sought out, but because of your individuality. That is why vanity best clothes a frivolous beauty.

861. It is stupid to run down your enemy before his death, infamous to do it after your victory.

862. The difficult problem for ambitious people to solve is to admit the merits of their older contemporaries and not to allow their shortcomings to impede them.

863. The radical evil: that everybody wants to be what they might and could be, and all the rest of mankind to be nothing, indeed, not to exist at all.

864. A person doesn't reveal his character until he talks about a great man or about something extraordinary. This is the real touchstone that shows up base copper metal.

865. Only people unable to produce anything themselves feel there is nothing there.

866. Why do we hear such everlastingly negative talk! People all imagine they'll be giving something away if they recognize the least bit of merit.

867. Of merit one demands modesty; but those who ostentatiously run down merit are listened to with relish.

868. People hate what they believe they have not themselves achieved; which is why the party spirit is so zealous. Every silly man imagines he is doing wonders, and this is how crowds of people who are nothing turn into something.

869. Provincial towns are egoistic; they imagine themselves to be the centre of things.

870. There is no one who is capable of realizing that anyone who works to construct or to protect does so in the interests of a party spirit.

871. In the heyday of one's life one has to put up with a great deal, either from what is out of date, or what is too new.

872. To what lengths have the Germans not gone to fend off what I may perhaps have managed to do and accomplish, and are they not still doing this? Had they accepted it all as of value, and then proceeded further, had they made capital out of my earnings, they would be further on than they in fact now are.

873. It is quite natural that scientists cannot altogether agree with me, there being so many different ways of thinking: I too will go on trying to put across my own point of view. But it is now the fashion to argue and work against me even in the aesthetic and moral field. I know very well wherefrom and whereto, why and wherefore, but will not be more explicit on the subject. The friends with whom I have lived, for whom I have lived, will know how to maintain their own position and also keep me in remembrance.

874. They can have a negative effect on opinion, but cannot prevent influence.

875. Tolerance should really only be a passing attitude: it should lead to appreciation. To tolerate is to offend.

876. Appreciation is the true form of liberality.

877. It isn't possible to remain on bad terms for long with truly like-minded people: some time or other you get together again; it's useless to try and keep the peace with people who are really of a different mind: every now and then things fall apart again.

878. I'm on good terms with all the people who are my immediate concern, and as to the rest, I won't go on putting up with things from them, and that's the end of the matter.

879. The whole year round I hear everybody talk in ways counter to my own opinions; so why shouldn't I say what I think for once in a while?

880. Even a truth, repeated, loses its charm, but an error repeated is altogether revolting.

881. Everybody puts up with what is absurd, false, because it insinuates itself; this doesn't apply to what is true, outspoken, because it excludes.

882. There are people who ponder about their friends' shortcomings: there's nothing to be gained by that. I have always been on the look-out for the merits of my opponents and this has been rewarding.

883. Reasonable and unreasonable things suffer the same opposition.

884. It's irrelevant whether what one says is true or false: both will be contradicted.

885. Opponents believe they are refuting us when they repeat their own opinion and take no notice of ours.

886. People who contradict and quarrel ought to bear in mind that not every language is intelligible to every person.

887. For surely everyone only hears what he understands.

888. A right answer is like a loving kiss.

889. There are many people who imagine that what they experience they also understand.

890. Who can say he is learning by experience if he is not the kind of person who does, in fact, have experiences?

891. One should only treat verbally about the most important matters concerning our feelings, our experience and also our thinking. Once a word has been uttered it immediately dies unless it is kept alive by a further word suitable to the person who is listening. Just pay attention to sociable conversation! If the word isn't already dead by the time it reaches the other person, he immediately proceeds to murder it by contradictions, diversions, side-stepping and whatever else you like to call the thousand varieties of unmannerliness in conversation. The written word is in an even worse situation. People don't want to read anything except that with which they are already to some extent familiar; what they want is what they know, they want a new way of putting what they are used to. But the written word does have the advantage over the spoken word in that it has permanence and can await the time when it will be allowed to have its effect.

892. What is expressed by word of mouth must be dedicated to the present, to the moment; what is written down should be dedicated to what is far away, to what is yet to come.

893. Do not ask whether we are in complete agreement, but whether we are acting with one mind.

894. I have found nothing more distressing than to be on bad terms with someone with whom I would have liked to act in agreement, be of one mind.

895. For the process of destruction all false arguments are valid, but by no means for that of construction. What is not true does not construct.

896. The present world does not deserve that we should do anything for it; for the world as it now is can disappear in a moment. We must work for the world that is gone and for the one yet to come; for the former so as to recognize its due merit, for the latter so that we may strive to heighten its worth.

897. For how many years do we have to do things in order to have at least some idea of *what* is to be done, and *how*!

898. Nothing is more terrible to watch than unremitting activity without any real basic foundation. Happy are those who are based, and know how to base themselves, in the realm of practical endeavour! But this calls for a quite special double capacity.

899. Nothing is more illogical than the most absolute illogicality, because this gives rise to unnatural phenomena which, in the end, change completely.

900. If you miss the first buttonhole, you can't ever get fully buttoned up.

901. You never go further than when you no longer know where you are going.

902. A man who spends his life doing something which he finally realizes is unproductive hates his occupation yet cannot get rid of it.

903. And let everyone consider carefully which of his faculties stand a chance of being effective in his own time and day.

904. Even a shabby camel can carry the load of many donkeys.

905. The person who wants to do better than everybody else is generally deceiving himself: he is just doing all he can and then is pleased to fancy that this is as much and more than everybody else can do.

906. Try to consolidate your own authority: it is established wherever there is mastery.

907. Let no one imagine that people have been waiting for him as a saviour!

908. Anyone who wants to be active and busy need only consider what ought to be done at any given moment and in this way he can proceed without diffusing his energies. This is where women are at an advantage, provided they understand it.

909. The present moment is a sort of public: you have to deceive it so that it imagines you are doing something; then it leaves you alone and secretly gets on with what its descendants will surely view with astonishment.

910. One single day is an altogether miserable unit; if you don't come to grips with a lustrum, you never harvest a full sheaf.

911. A day belongs to the domain of error and mistakes, a sequence of time to success and achievement.

912. He who looks ahead is lord of the day.

913. I curse the daily round, because it's always absurd. But what we can wrest from it by our effort may possibly add up to something in the end.

914. At times when a monstrous fate overwhelms us and we hardly look up or look round to see what can be done and in what direction we are to deploy our powers and activity to best advantage, and we need the greatest enthusiasm of a kind that can only endure if it isn't too empirical – at such times our day by day efforts are being attacked, not, maybe, by dragons, but by miniature dragons in the shape of rag-and-bone maggots.

915.   The whole of life consists of
                       wanting and not-succeeding,
                       succeeding and not-wanting.

916. Wanting and succeeding is not worthwhile – or can be annoying to speak of.

917. The lives of many people consist of gossip, action and intrigue, all in aid of momentary effects.

918. If monkeys could reach the point of being bored, they could turn into human beings.

919. Clever people find life easy when fools find it hard, and often it's hard for the clever and easy for the fool.

920. It is better to let folly proceed without interference rather than try to remedy it by reasoning. Reason loses its power when fused with folly, and folly thereby forfeits its own nature which often helps it along.

921. The world is hardly helped by ideas which did not take their origin from nature in action and which also fail to react beneficially on active life; this brings about a constant ebb and flow, a manifold interchange in harmony with the circumstances of life at any given point.

922. In the practical sphere relentless intelligence is reason – because the highest achievement of reason, that is, *vis-à-vis* intelligence, is to make intelligence relentless.

923. False tendencies are a kind of real longing, more advantageous, at any rate, than a false tendency expressed as an ideal longing.

924. All practical people try to make the world something they can manipulate by hand; all thinkers want it to suit their head. Let them see how far each can succeed.

925. The realistically minded: what has not been accomplished finds no demand. The idealistically minded: what is being demanded can't be accomplished forthwith.

926. In the ideal realm all depends on bursts of enthusiasm; in the real world what matters is perseverance.

927. The most curious thing in life is our trustful belief that others will guide us. If we lack this trust, we lurch and tumble along our own way; if we have it, then before we know what's happening, we're also being very badly misled.

928. The very worst kind of culture a man can give himself is the conviction that other people don't take any notice of him.

929. Who ought to have had patience with me if I hadn't had any myself?

930. People think one ought to be busy with them when one isn't busy with oneself.

931. A scorched child shuns the fire; an old man who has been scorched is afraid to warm himself.

932. How very effective practice can be! Spectators shout and the defeated man is silent.

933. How good it would have been for us if only we had understood or been told earlier that one is never on better terms with a woman friend than when praising our rival. For then her heart opens up, every fear of hurting you, her worry that she might lose you, has vanished; she takes you into her confidence and you are happy in the conviction that you will pick the fruit from the tree if you're affable enough to let others have the falling leaves.

934. If there's some matter which displeases me, I just leave it alone or I make a better job of it.

935. Whoever descends deep down into himself will always realize he is only half a being; let him find a girl or a world, no matter which, and he will become a whole.

936. Does the sparrow know how the stork feels?

937. The tiger who wants to make the stag understand how delicious it is to swallow draughts of blood.

938. Healthy people are those in whose bodily and intellectual organization each part has a '*vita propria*', a life of its own.

939. We're only really thinking when we can't think out fully what we are thinking about!

940. If wise men didn't make mistakes, fools would have to despair.

941. Some people are proud about what they know; about what they don't know, they are arrogant.

942. A man who wants to take up some branch of learning will necessarily be deceived or he will deceive himself unless he is irresistibly determined by external demands. Who would be a medical doctor if he had a complete picture of all the trials that are in store for him?

943. The historian cannot and need not achieve absolute certainties; even mathematicians cannot explain why the comet of 1779, which should have returned in five or eleven years, has not, as yet, appeared.

944. It is the same with history as with nature, as with all profound problems, whether past, present or future: the more deeply and seriously one enters into problems, the more difficult are those that arise. If you are unafraid and forge ahead boldly, you increase in stature and feel intellectually furthered and more at ease.

945. History, like the universe which it is said to represent, has a real and an ideal aspect.

946. Credit belongs to the ideal side of things, physical power to what is real.

947. Credit is an idea of reliability brought about by real achievements.

948. Ownership is a clumsy concept and it is good that there should be discussion about it, *ne incerta sint rerum dominia* [lest uncertainty should prevail].

949. Every human being feels privileged.
  This feeling is contravened

> (1) by the necessity of nature,
> (2) by society.

re 1. Human beings cannot escape this, avoid it, gain from it. All we can do is to comply by means of diet, not forestalling it.
  re 2. Human beings cannot escape this, nor avoid it; but provided we renounce our sense of privilege, we can ensure that society gives us a share in its benefits.

950. The highest aim of society is the consequence of benefits assured to everyone. Each sensible member, and of course society itself, sacrifices a good deal for this consequence. Living out this consequence means the almost total annulment of the members' momentary benefit.

951. In society everyone is equal. No society can be founded on anything but the concept of equality, and certainly not on that of liberty. Equality is what I want to find in society; liberty, that is, moral liberty, my willingness to submit, this is my own personal contribution.

952. So the society which I join must say to me: 'You are to be like all the rest of us.' But it can only add: 'We would also wish you to be free,' that is to say, we wish you to make use of your privileges in a spirit of conviction, by your own free and reasonable will.

953. Law-givers or revolutionaries who promise both equality and freedom at one and the same time are either dreamers or charlatans.

954. Imaginary equality: the first way to show inequality in action.

955. Every revolution ends in a state of nature devoid of law and shame (Picards, Anabaptists, Sansculottes).

956. As soon as tyranny comes to an end, it is immediately replaced by conflict between aristocracy and democracy.

957. People are to be seen as organs of their century who, as a rule, act unconsciously.

958. A fault of Enlightenment, so called: it gives many-sidedness to people whose one-sided condition one cannot alter.

959. Before the Revolution all was zealous endeavour; after it all was transformed into demands.

960. In some states, as a result of the violent and compulsive upheavals they have lived through, there has been a certain exaggeration in the educational sphere whose damaging effects are even now being more generally acknowledged by competent, upright principals of such institutions. Excellent men live in a kind of despair because they consider as useless and harmful what their office and rules oblige them to teach and pass on to posterity.

961. Nothing is sadder than to watch the absolute urge for the unconditional in this altogether conditional world; perhaps in the year 1830 it seems even more unsuitable than ever.

962. No state can endure the condition of being at the same time armed and on the defensive.

963. Can a state become mature? This is a strange question. I would reply 'yes', provided all men could be born at the age of thirty; but as youth will eternally be forward and age not forward enough, the man who really is mature will always be trapped between the two and will have to struggle along in a strange way, getting by as best he can.

964. A great prerogative: to be understanding, indeed reasonable, not only in one's private affairs, for everyone knows that, but also in public.

965. Majesty is the possibility and power to do right or wrong without regard to reward or punishment.

966. To rule and to enjoy don't go together. To enjoy means to belong light-heartedly to oneself and to others; to rule means to do good in the most seriously purposeful way to oneself and to others.

967. It is easy to learn how to rule, hard to learn how to reign.

968. If you have clear concepts, you know how to give orders.

969. What monarchs publish in newspapers doesn't read well; for power should act, not talk. What liberals put forward is always readable; for if a man has been defeated because he cannot act, he at least wants to air his views by talking. 'Let them sing, if only they pay up!' said Mazarin when he was shown satirical songs about a new tax.

970. If you haven't been reading the newspapers for a few months and then read them all together, you realize how much time is wasted with these sheets of paper. The world has always been divided into parties, and this applies more especially nowadays; and whenever there is a situation of uncertainty, the journalist baits either one party or the other, either more or less, and boosts our inner preference or dislike from one day to the next until, in the end, there is a decision and then, what has happened is an object of wonder, as though it were an act of God.

971. All official news in the papers is stilted; the rest is flat.

972. None clamour for freedom of the press except those who want to misuse it.

973. In recent times Germans have assumed that freedom of the press is nothing more than being free to cast scorn on one another in public.

974. In times gone by Germans rejoiced solely in the fact that no one was constrained to obey others.

975. Justice: a characteristic and an illusion of the Germans.

976. The real German is many-sided in the culture and unity of his character.

977. Englishmen will shame us by their plain common sense and good will, Frenchmen by witty discretion and practical expertise.

978. A German should learn all languages so that no foreigner could discomfort him at home and he himself could be at home everywhere when abroad.

979. The effective power of a language does not consist in rejecting but in assimilating what is alien.

980. I curse all negative purism decreeing that we should banish a foreign word which expresses a great deal or what is more subtle.

981. I stand for affirmative purism which is productive and based solely on the question: where do we have to use circumlocution while our neighbour has a single incisive word?

982. Pedantic purism is an absurd rejection of a wider extension of significance and spirit (e.g. the English word 'grief').

983. No word stands still, but usage is always shifting it from its original place to a lower rather than a higher position, changing it for the worse rather than the better, narrowing the scope rather than extending it, and the mutability of words allows us to understand the mutability of concepts.

984. Philologists: Apollo Sauroktonos, always on the watch with his pointed little stylus at the ready to spear a lizard.

985. There is not much difference between misunderstanding a correct passage and imputing some meaning or other to a corrupt passage. This last is more profitable for an individual than the first. It constitutes a private emendation by which a man gains for his own spirit what the first has gained for the letter of the text.

986. What we call fashion is momentary transmission. Every form of transmission involves a certain need to put oneself on the same level as what is being handed down.

987. As one grows older one must consciously, at some particular point, call a halt.

988. It is not fitting for an aged person to yield to fashion, either in his way of thinking or in his dress.

989. But one must know where one stands and where others are heading.

990. It's the same with the years of our life as with the Sibylline books: the more of them you burn, the more cherished they become.

991. If youth be a fault, it is one soon discarded.

992. To have timely insight, when you are young, into the advantages of age, and to preserve the advantages of youth when you are old – both are one and the same bliss.

993. There is no self-deception when a young man has great expectations. But just as, in the past, he felt hope in his heart, so too he must look for fulfilment not outside himself but in his heart.

994. 'I stumbled over the roots of a tree I had myself planted.' The forester who said that must have been an old man.

995. To think that Man finally turns into an 'epitomator'! And to get as far as that is happy enough.

996. Parents and children have no choice but to die either before or after one another, and in the end it's hard to tell which ought to be preferred.

997. When I think about my death I may not, I cannot think about what organization is then being destroyed.

998. In every great parting there lies a seed of insanity; one must beware of brooding over it and nurturing it in one's thinking.

999. It is most remarkable that what is left over from a human being is two opposite entities: the casing and skeletal framework in and with which the spirit resided here on earth, and the ideal effects which emanated from this by word and deed.

1000. A spoken word demands itself in reply.

1001.   Mysticism: immature poetry, immature philosophy.
Poetry: a mature nature.
Philosophy: a mature reason.

1002. Poetry points to the mysteries of nature and tries to unriddle them by imagery;

philosophy points to the mysteries of reason and tries to unriddle them by the word (philosophy of nature, experimental philosophy);

mysticism points to the mysteries of nature and of reason and tries to unriddle them by word and image.

1003. Symbolical imagination: domain of poetry; hypothetical explanation: domain of philosophy.

1004.   Truth (general), recognized and held by us;
passion (specific), which hinders and holds us;
the third factor, what is rhetorical, vacillating between truth
and passion.

1005. Mood is something unconscious and is based on sensuality. It is the contradiction of sensuality with itself.

1006. Humour arises when reason is not in a state of balance with things, but strives to dominate them and fails: this is cross or bad humour; or there's the kind which to some extent subjects itself to circumstances and is open to play, *salvo honore*: and this is merry or good humour. It can well be symbolized by a father who condescends to play with his children and gets more fun than he gives. In this case reason acts the buffoon, in the former case the melancholy clown.

1007. Genius practises a kind of ubiquity, reaching out towards generality before experience, and afterwards to what is particular.

1008. Good fortune of genius: to be born in serious times.

1009. Greatly talented people are the most attractive medium of reconciliation.

1010. A broad-minded man of genius strives to be in advance of his century; a talented man of obstinate nature often wants to retard his century.

1011. Acumen is least likely to desert clever men when they are in the wrong.

1012. The most dreadful thing of all is when dull, incapable men team up with dreamers divorced from reality.

1013. One is bound to admit that the German world, boasting, as it does, many people of good and admirable intelligence, is becoming ever more disunited and confused in art and science, in historical, theoretical and practical matters.

1014. If one did not look with reverence on art and science as something eternal, a living and complete whole in itself, compounded of merits and failings, one would be at a loss and grieved that wealth can cause such embarrassment.

1015. What kind of an age is this when one has to envy those who are buried?

1016. What is not original is unimportant and what is original is always marked by the frailties of the individual.

1017. If one can't improve on something, one can at least do it differently; this is the preferred solution of listeners and readers who traditionally regard one another with indifference.

1018. There's so much talk about taste: taste consists of euphemisms. These spare the ear and excite the mind.

1019. The public wants to be treated like women: on no account must they be told anything except what they want to hear.

1020. The public would rather complain incessantly about how badly it is served than take any trouble to ensure better service.

1021. There are empirical enthusiasts who, though rightly enough, wax ecstatic about good new productions as though nothing more perfect had ever been produced the world over.

1022. Great damage is done by false ideas arising from the general public, because the value of works already in existence is immediately underestimated if they do not happen to fit in to the pattern of current prejudice.

1023. There is no vantage point within an epoch from out of which an epoch can be considered and assessed.

1024. No nation can judge rightly except about what is done and written within its own domain. The same could be said about every epoch.

1025. True judgements embracing all epochs and all nations are very rare.

1026. No nation can rightly exercise criticism except on the basis of having outstanding, competent and distinguished works to its credit.

1027. Criticism is like Ate: she pursues authors, but she limps.

1028. What is true, good and excellent is also simple and always the same in itself, however it makes its appearance. What is erroneous, however, and invites censure, is most manifold, diverse in itself, battling not only against what is good and true, but also against its own self, at loggerheads within. This is why, in all literature, expressions of adverse criticism must always exceed words of praise.

1029. With the Greeks, where poetry and rhetoric were simple we find approval more often than disapproval; with the Latins, however, it is the other way round, and the more poetry and rhetoric degenerate, the more will censure increase and praise dwindle.

1030. Literature only degenerates in the same measure that people themselves degenerate.

1031. What is Classical is healthy; what is Romantic is sick.

1032. Ovid remained Classical even in his exile: he does not look for his distress in himself, but in his exile from the capital city of the world.

1033. What is Romantic has already lost its way in its own abyss; one can hardly imagine anything more horrible than its quite disgusting recent productions.

1034. The English and French have outdone us in this respect. Bodies which rot while still physically alive and are edified by the detailed contemplation of their own decay, dead people who remain alive for the corruption of others and who nourish their deadness on living substance – that's the state our producers have reached!

1035. In Antiquity things of this kind only haunt the scene as rare diseases; nowadays they have become endemic and epidemic.

1036. Sakuntala: here the poet appears in his most elevated function. As the representative of the most natural condition, of the most refined life-style, the purest moral endeavour, the most dignified majesty and the most serious worship of God, he dares to enter into a realm of the most vulgar and ridiculous contrasts.

1037. Somebody said: 'Why do you bother about Homer? Especially since you don't understand him?' I don't understand the sun, the moon, the stars high above my head, and I recognize myself in them even as I look at them and contemplate their wonderful regular course, wondering as I gaze whether I too might one day come to some good.

1038. That the fine arts are so highly rated in the *Iliad* might well amount to an argument for the modernity of the poem.

1039. Let the Moderns write in Latin when they have to structure something out of nothing. If they don't, then all they achieve is to turn their small 'something' into nothing.

1040. The Latin language has a kind of imperative of authorship.

1041. Among the happy circumstances which developed Shakespeare's great inborn talent in a free and clear way, there is also the fact that he was a Protestant; otherwise he would have had to glorify absurdities as did Kalidasa and Calderón.

1042. Henry the Fourth by Shakespeare: if everything of this kind that had ever been written and come down to our time had been lost, a perfect reconstruction of poetry and rhetoric would be possible by means of this drama.

1043. In order to whip up the old, most insipid commonplaces of mankind, Klopstock enlisted heaven and hell, sun, moon and stars, time and eternity, God and the devil.

1044. Schmidt von Werneuchen is the truly natural character. Everybody has made fun of him, and rightly so; and yet it wouldn't have been possible to make fun of him had he not had real merit as a poet, and this deserves our respect.

1045. Eulenspiegel: all the main jokes of the book are based on the fact that everybody talks in figures of speech and Eulenspiegel understands all this literally.

1046. Fairytale: presents impossible events under possible or almost impossible conditions as though they were possible.

1047. Novel: presents possible events under impossible or almost impossible conditions as though they were real.

1048. The hero in a novel assimilates everything; the hero in the theatre does not have to find anything similar in what is all around him.

1049. The fragments of Aristotle's treatise on poetical art are wonderful to contemplate. If we know the theatre inside out like those of us who have spent a significant part of our life on this art form and have done a great deal of work in this field, we come to realize that we must first of all familiarize ourselves with this man's philosophical cast of mind. This then helps us to grasp his understanding of this art form; our study, moreover, only serves to confuse us, if, as in the case of modern poetics, only the most surface aspects of his teaching have been applied, and that to their own destruction.

1050. The tragedian's real duty and task is to show and demonstrate in an intelligible experiment a psychological and moral phenomenon dating from the past.

1051. What are called motives are, in fact, phenomena of the spirit of man which have recurred and will do so again, and are only shown and demonstrated by the poet as being historical.

1052. It takes genius to create a dramatic work. Sensibility is to be dominant at the end, reason in the middle and understanding at the beginning, while, throughout, all is to be declaimed evenly with the help of vividly clear imaginative power.

1053. Nothing is theatrical which the eye could not see as symbolical.

1054. Theatre criticism of the usual kind is a merciless catalogue of sins accusingly presented to poor malefactors by an evil spirit and without a helping hand to point to a better way.

1055. A romance is not a legal action where there has to be a definitive judgement.

1056. When one is translating one has to go right up to the untranslatable; but it is only at this point that one actually discovers the foreign nation and the foreign language.

1057. It makes a big difference whether I read for enjoyment and stimulus or for knowledge and instruction.

1058. There are books which tell us all and yet leave us understanding nothing about the matter in the end.

1059. If a dictionary can catch up with an author, he is no good.

1060. When I see a misprint I always imagine that there has been some new invention.

1061. Publishers have declared themselves, as well as authors, to be above the law; how then do they propose to judge among themselves, and who will want to go to law with them?

1062. Longing which soars away into the distance, but confines its melody within itself, creates the minor key.

1063. Cantilena: eternalizing the fullness of love and of all passionate bliss.

On Art and Art History: Aphorisms for the Attention of Friends and Opponents

1064. Anyone who now intends to write or argue about art ought to have some idea of what philosophy has achieved and continues to achieve in our day.

1065. Whoever wants to accuse an author of obscurity ought first of all to have a good look at his own inward self and see whether it is really light in there: twilight makes even very clear handwriting impossible to read.

1066. Whoever wants to enter into an argument must be careful not to say things which no one is arguing about anyway.

1067. Whoever wants to enter into argument about maxims should be capable of setting them up very clearly and of doing battle in the light of this clarity; he will otherwise run the danger of fighting against his own home-made phantoms.

1068. The obscurity of certain maxims is only relative: it doesn't do to make everything that is obvious to a practitioner crystal-clear to a listener.

1069. An artist who produces valuable work is not always capable of giving a reasoned account of his own achievements or those of others.

1070. It isn't possible to separate nature and idea without destroying art as well as life.

1071. When artists talk about nature, they always have the notion of an 'idea' at the back of their mind, without being clearly conscious of this fact.

1072. The same goes for all who stress the need for experience; they don't realize that experiential knowledge is only one half of experience.

1073. First we hear about nature and imitation of nature; then we get on to what is supposed to be 'beautiful nature'. One has to make a choice. The best, presumably! And how is this to be recognized? What norm is to inform our choice? And where is the norm? Surely not in nature too?

1074. And suppose that the subject had been agreed, the most beautiful tree in the forest, one which the forester, too, had pronounced to be a perfect one of its kind. Now in order to transform the tree into a picture I walk round it and look for its most beautiful aspect. I step far enough away to survey it completely, I wait till the light is favourable, and by now a great deal of the 'tree-in-nature' is supposed to have got as far as the sketch-block!

1075. The layman may believe this; the artist from behind the painted stage scenery and the wings of his art should be more enlightened.

1076. Precisely that which uneducated people single out as 'nature' in a work of art is not nature (from the outside), but a human being (nature from the inside).

1077. We know of no world except that in relation to human beings; we want no art except that which is the imprint of that relationship.

1078. He who was the first to fix the vanishing points of the manifold play of horizontal lines on to his horizon invented the principle of perspective.

1079. He who was the first to develop the harmony of colours out of the systole and diastole to which the retina is formed, out of the syncrisis and diacrisis, to speak with Plato, invented the principle of coloration.

1080. Look within yourselves and you will find everything, and rejoice that out there, by whatever name you may call it, there is nature which says an unconditional yes, assenting to all that you have found within yourselves!

1081. Quite a number of things may have been invented, discovered long ago, and yet fail to be of influence in this world; things may influence and yet remain unnoticed, may influence yet fail to reach general effectiveness. Which is why every story of an invention has to grapple with the most extraordinary conundrums.

1082. It is just as hard to learn something from models as from nature itself.

1083. Form as well as matter has to be digested, and it is in fact much harder to digest.

1084. Some have studied on the model of Antiquity and have not quite managed to grasp its essence; does that make them culpable?

1085. Higher demands, even unfulfilled, are in themselves more worthy of esteem than lower demands completely fulfilled.

1086. Dry naïvety, stiff worthiness, anxious uprightness and however else you may want to characterize German art are to be found in every earlier simpler art form. You can also see them in the older Venetians, Florentines, and so on.

1087. And are we Germans only to see ourselves as original if we don't rise above our beginnings?

1088. And just because Albrecht Dürer with his incomparable talent could never rise to the idea of the harmony of beauty, nor even to the idea of fitting purpose, are we to stay stuck to the soil for ever?

1089. Albrecht Dürer's development was helped by a most deeply realistic way of seeing the world, by a kindly compassion for the whole of the present human condition in all its aspects; what did him damage was a gloomy imagination of a form- and fathomless kind.

1090. How Martin Schongauer compares with him, and how in his case

German achievement is more limited, would make an interesting and useful comparison, showing that no decision can yet be reached in this matter.

1091. If only the butterfly would emerge from every chrysalis in all schools of Italian painting!

1092. Are we to crawl around for ever as caterpillars just because a few nordic artists find this of advantage?

1093. Now that Klopstock has delivered us from rhyme and Voss has given us patterns of prosody, are we really to revert to primitive verse patterns like those of Hans Sachs?

1094. Do let's be versatile! German turnips taste good, best of all mixed with chestnuts, and these choice things flourish at a far distance from one another.

1095. Do allow us oriental and southern forms as well as western and nordic ones in our collections of miscellaneous works!

1096. One is only versatile if one strives (in real earnest) for the highest because one has to, and descends (for fun) to lesser levels because one wants to.

1097. Do leave German poets the pious wish to count as followers of Homer! German sculptors, it won't do you any harm to set your hearts on fame as the last followers of Praxiteles!

1098. How hard an artist has to study if he is to see a peach as Huysum saw it! So shouldn't we make the attempt to see human beings as the Greeks saw them?

1099. Those who need to take proportion (what can be measured) from Antiquity should not pour scorn on us because we want to take from Antiquity what cannot be measured.

1100. It is quite enough that lovers of art unanimously agree in recognizing and appreciating what is perfect; about what is of middling quality, argument can never end.

1101. All that is significant – and that alone constitutes the excellence of a work of art – is not given recognition; all that is fruitful and positive is disregarded; no one easily understands a profoundly comprehensive synthesis.

1102. You select a pattern and with that you mix your individuality: that's the sum total of your art. There's no thought of any principles, any school, any follow-on; everything is arbitrary and according to each one's fancy. Liberating yourself from laws which are only hallowed by tradition, nothing can be said against that; but not to consider that there really must be laws which arise from the very nature of every art – that doesn't occur to anyone.

1103. Every good and bad work of art belongs to nature as soon as it has been produced. Antiquity belongs to nature, and, indeed, if it evokes response, it belongs to nature at its most natural, and we are not to study this noble nature, but only its common form!

1104. For it is really commonness which these gentlemen regard as nature! To draw on one's own resources may well mean dealing with what we can comfortably manage!

1105. Art: another nature, mysterious too, but more intelligible; for it originates in reason.

1106. Nature works by laws which it laid down for itself in harmony with the creator; art works by rules about which it has come to terms with genius.

1107. Art is based on a kind of religious sense, on a deep and unassailable seriousness, which is why it's so much inclined to a link with religion. Religion has no need of a sense for art, it rests on its own seriousness; but neither does it impart a sense for, nor any degree of taste for, art.

1108. Reality in its highest degree of usefulness (appropriateness) will also be beautiful.

1109. Perfection is already there when what is necessary is already being accomplished; beauty is there when what is necessary is accomplished but hidden.

1110. Perfection can exist together with disproportion; beauty only with proportion.

1111. Works of art are destroyed as soon as artistic sense disappears.

1112. Allegory transforms an object of perception into a concept, the concept into an image, but in such a way that the concept continues to remain circumscribed and completely available and expressible within the image.

1113. Symbolism transforms an object of perception into an idea, the idea into an image, and does it in such a way that the idea always remains infinitely operative and unattainable so that even if it is put into words in all languages, it still remains inexpressible.

1114. In Rembrandt's fine etching of Christ driving buyers and sellers out of the temple, the circle of light which usually surrounds the Lord's head has been transferred, as it were, into his outstretched hand lit up in shining splendour at its divine work and striking out powerfully. About his head, as also his face, there is darkness.

1115. Every great artist seizes hold of us, infects us. Everything in us which has the same kind of capacity stirs, and as we have some mental image of greatness and a certain disposition for it, we quite easily imagine that the same seed is at work within us.

1116. Everyone has temperament; some have a good disposition; understanding of art is rare.

1117. There is a certain stage in every art form which can be reached by natural talents, on one's own, so to speak. At the same time, however, it is impossible to go beyond this point if art does not come to our aid.

1118. We may well praise an artist by saying: all this comes out of his own self. If only I didn't have to listen to this yet again! Looking more closely, the products of an original genius of this kind are mostly reminiscences; any experienced person will usually be able to trace their origin one by one.

1119. 'Creating out of oneself', as it is called, usually results in false originals and mannerists.

1120. Why do we blame manneristic work so heavily, other than because we believe that turning away from it and getting on the right road is impossible?

1121. Art should not emphasize what is painful.

1122. What the last touch can do must already be clearly expressed by the first. This must already lay down what is finally to be done.

1123. 'You mustn't smell and sniff at my pictures – the colours are unhealthy' – Rembrandt.

1124. Even the best people don't always manage to structure a complete whole out of many sketches.

1125. Even a moderate talent is always perceptive in the presence of nature, which is why really careful drawings always give us pleasure.

1126. Cause of the dilettante approach: flight from mannerism, ignorance of method, the foolish enterprise of trying to do what is actually impossible, the kind of thing that would call for the most consummate art if one were ever able to get anywhere near it.

1127. Mistake of dilettantes: wanting forthwith to merge imagination and technique.

1128. There is a tradition that Daedalus, the first sculptor, was envious of the potter's invention of the wheel. Maybe it wasn't a question of envy; but the great man probably had a premonition that, in the long run, technique might well damage art.

1129. Technique in league with bad taste is the most fearsome enemy of art.

1130. In connection with the Berlin pattern or model pictures for manufacturers, the question arose whether the extremely careful drawing of these sheets had really been warranted; but it then transpired that it was precisely the talented young artist and craftsman for whom the execution of these designs had the greatest appeal, and that studying and copying such models was what really enabled him to understand the work as a whole and the high worth of its forms.

1131. Chodowiecki is a most respectable, and we may say, ideally minded artist. His good works always show spirit and taste. Nothing more ideal could be expected of the circle in which he worked.

1132. The most terrible thing for the student is that, in the end, he does have to re-establish his own stance as against his master. The more vigorous the latter's contribution, the greater the discontent, indeed the despair, of the one at the receiving end.

1133. A noble philosopher described architecture as frozen music and as a result had to watch much negative head-shaking. We believe this beautiful idea cannot be more aptly resurrected than by calling architecture music that has merged into silence.

Imagine Orpheus, when he was assigned a great desolate building site, shrewdly settling at the most appropriate spot and forming a large market place all around him by the life-giving music of his lyre. Rocky stones, rapidly reft from their massive blocks by the powerful command, the friendly enticement of music, were compelled to form an artistic and craftsman-like structure in their enthusiastic approach, and make up a fitting and orderly pattern of rhythmic stacks and walls. And in this way street may be added to street! Nor will strong protective walls be lacking.

The sound of the music dies away but the harmony remains. The citizens of a town of this kind walk and work surrounded by eternal melodies; the spirit cannot sink, action cannot fall asleep, the eye takes over the function, the due work, the duty of the ear, and on the most ordinary day the citizens feel they are in an ideal state; without taking thought, without inquiring into causes, they enter into the highest ethical and religious delight. Make a habit of walking up and down in St Peter's basilica and you will feel an analogue of what we have dared to put into words.

The citizen of a badly built town, on the other hand, where fate has swept the houses together with a slack broom, unknowingly lives in a desert of dismal conditions; a stranger entering it feels as though he were listening to bagpipes, whistles and tambourines and would soon have to be watching bear dances and leaping monkeys.

1134. The temples of Antiquity concentrate God in man; medieval churches strive upward to God on high.

On Nature and Natural Science

1135. A concept is summation, an idea is the result of experience; to arrive at the former you need understanding, at the latter reasoning power.

1136. What is termed an idea: that which always becomes apparent and is therefore evident to us as the law of all appearances.

1137. Idea and appearance only coincide in the highest and in the most communal sphere; they separate in all the intermediate stages of contemplation and experience. The highest stage is seeing as identical what is different; the most communal stage is doing, actively linking as identical what is divided.

1138. What so very much confounds us, when we have to admit the existence of the idea in its manifestation, is that it often, indeed usually, contradicts the senses. The system of Copernicus rested on an idea that was hard to grasp and still contradicts our senses every day. We just repeat what we don't recognize or understand. Similarly, the metamorphosis of plants contradicts our senses.

1139. The sublime, gradually divided into separate entities as we grow in knowledge, does not readily merge again in our mind; this means that we are deprived in stages of the best thing granted to us, of the sense of oneness which lifts us up completely into sharing a sense of the infinite; and, on the other hand, we are all the time diminishing in stature as we grow in knowledge. Whereas before we were like giants in view of the whole, we now see ourselves as dwarfs in the face of separate sections.

1140. It is a pleasant occupation to inquire into nature and into one's own self at the same time, not to force either nature or one's own spirit, but to bring both into a balanced relationship by a gentle reciprocal influence.

1141. Putting oneself on a par with objects in breadth means learning; understanding objects in depth means invention.

1142. What you invent you do with love; what you have learnt you do with certainty.

1143. What actually is invention? It is the conclusion of what has been sought.

1144. What is the difference between an axiom and an enthymeme? An axiom: what we want to admit from the beginning without proof; an enthymeme: what reminds us of many cases and links together individual items we have already realized.

1145. No one can rob us of the joy of a first moment of perception, of discovery so called. But if we expect honour as well, this can be very minimal, for as a rule we're not the first.

1146. And what does invention really mean, and who can say that he has invented this or that? And it is in any case sheer folly to harp on priority; for it's just mindless conceit if one doesn't want to admit honestly to plagiarism.

1147. Together with standpoints when they disappear from the world, the viewed objects themselves are often lost. For, in a higher sense, one can say that the standpoint is the object.

1148. Much more than one thinks has already been discovered. As objects are only lifted out of nothingness by a human point of view, so when the points of view vanish, the objects, too, return to nothingness: rounding of the earth, Plato's theory of blueness.

1149. Two feelings most difficult to get over: to have found something that has already been found, and not to find something that one should have found.

1150. Thinking is more interesting than knowing, but not more interesting than contemplating.

1151. Knowing is based on discerning what is to be differentiated, scientific knowledge on what is not to be differentiated.

1152. Knowing is guided towards scientific knowledge as one becomes aware of the gaps in one's thinking, and by the feeling of one's shortcomings which persists before, with, and after all knowing.

1153. In knowing and thinking things out there is both what is false and what is true. And as this then takes on the aspect of scientific knowledge, it turns into a being that looks both true and false.

1154. We would not describe our knowledge as piecework if we had not got a basic notion of totality.

1155. The sciences as well as the arts consist of what can be handed down and learnt (the real part) and of what cannot be handed down or learnt (the ideal part).

1156. In the history of the sciences the ideal part has a different relationship to the real part than is the case in the rest of world history.

1157. The history of the sciences: phenomena are the 'real' part, views about phenomena the 'ideal'.

1158. Four epochs in the sciences:

> *childlike:*
> poetical, superstitious
> *empirical:*
> questioning, curious
> *dogmatic:*
> didactic, pedantic
> *idealistic:*
> methodical, mystic

1159. 'Only present science belongs to us, not what is past nor what is yet to come.'

1160. In the sixteenth century the sciences don't belong to this individual or to another, but to the world. The world has the sciences, owns them; all the individual man does is to take possession of all this wealth.

1161. The sciences are self-destructive in double fashion: by their wide coverage and by the depth which they explore.

1162. As all the demands made on the sciences are so tremendous, it is most understandable that nothing whatever is achieved.

1163. What most retards the development of the sciences is that those who pursue them are so unequal intellectually.

1164. Where feeble intellects go wrong in their thinking is that they proceed immediately from the single factor to what is general, whereas it is only in totality that what is general can be sought.

1165. In the history of research into nature it is most noticeable that observers are too quick to rush towards theory, and that this makes them inadequate, hypothetical.

1166. An epoch in the experimental sciences dates from Lord Bacon of Verulam. Their progress has, however, often been traversed and made unviable by theoretical tendencies. Strictly speaking, every single day could and should be the start of a new epoch.

1167. The century has moved on; all the same, each individual starts again from the beginning.

1168. We have reason to sort out our experience each and every day and to clear out our mind.

1169. As those who start scientific experiments seldom know what they really want and what is to be the end result, they mostly pursue their way with great zeal; soon, however, as nothing decisive really seems to be happening, they let the enterprise go and even try to make it suspect for others.

1170. Because in the second half of the seventeenth century such a very great debt to the microscope had been incurred, the beginning of the eighteenth century was intent on treating it disdainfully.

1171. As recent times had perfected meteorological observations to the highest point of accuracy, the attempt is now being made to banish them from northern regions and to allow them only to the observer in the Tropics.

1172. People have even got tired of, and regarded as something superfluous, sexuality which, considered from a higher point of view, is so greatly valuable, and attempts have been made to banish it! And the same thing is happening to older art history, where, for fifty years, people have put in carefully accurate study to discern the differences between epochs and their sequence! And now all this is supposed to have been futile and all periods as they follow one after the other are to be seen as identical and indistinguishable.

1173. Our advice is that everybody should keep to the road on which he has set out and on no account allow himself to be impressed by authority, constrained by general agreement and swayed by fashion.

1174. Authority: man cannot exist without it, and yet it involves as much error as truth. It eternalizes single factors that were meant to be no more than passing, it rejects and lets go what should have been kept, and is the main reason why humanity fails to move from the spot.

1175. The ordinary scholar considers that everything can be transmitted to posterity and fails to notice that the meanness of his views doesn't allow him to grasp what really can be transmitted.

1176. To one who is striving to get on, inadequacy is more inimical than one might imagine.

1177. Two things above all should be avoided: rigidity if you confine yourself to your subject, inadequacy if you leave its confines.

1178. If old people tend to slow up in the sciences, then it is also true to say that young people tend to retrogress. Old people will not acknowledge progress if there is no link with their earlier ideas; and this happens to young people if they are not up to a new idea and would yet have liked to achieve something extraordinary.

1179. They are certainly serious in their intention, but they don't know what they should do with their serious intent.

1180. They don't want to know anything about what they do understand.

1181. In New York there are ninety different Christian confessions, each and all acknowledge God and the Lord in their own particular way without really being at loggerheads with one another. We must get as far as that in nature study and indeed in every branch of research; for what sense is there in everybody talking about liberal attitudes and yet wanting to prevent others from thinking in their own way and having their own say?

1182. All individuals, and, if they are competent, all their followers, look on the problematic nature of the sciences as something for or against which one should do battle, just as if it were another view of life, while scientific knowledge calls for a solution, adjustment or for setting up antinomies which cannot be reconciled. This is also Aguillonius' case.

1183. If someone claims he has refuted me, he doesn't stop to think that all he is doing is to postulate a view contrary to mine; this doesn't as yet settle anything. A third person has the same right, and so on *ad infinitum.*

1184. In scientific disputes we must guard against multiplying problems.

1185. In the sciences, and in general, if one wants to cover the whole of anything, all that is finally left if this is to be complete is to make truth valid as against error, error against truth. A man cannot examine everything himself; he has to keep to what has been handed down, and if he wants a job, he has to pay homage to his patrons' views. Let all academic teachers examine their conscience in the light of this!

1186. The most worthy physics professor might well be a man who could completely demonstrate the nullity of his compendium and of his figures as compared with nature and the highest demands of the spirit.

1187. Not everything desirable is attainable; not everything that can be known is knowable.

1188. He who has the understanding to declare his limitations is closest to perfection.

1189. As people can't manage what is necessary, they take pains about what is useless.

1190. Animals are taught by means of their organs; man teaches his organs and controls them.

1191. Anaxagoras teaches that all animals have active reason but not passive reason, which is, as it were, the interpreter of understanding.

1192. The Ancients compare the hand with reason. Reason is the art of arts; the hand is the technical means of all craftsmanship.

1193. The senses don't deceive; judgement deceives.

1194. Man is sufficiently equipped for all truly earthly necessities if he trusts his senses and develops them in such a way that they go on being worthy of trust.

1195. No one contests the fact that vision is capable of estimating the distance between objects which are adjacent, or even above one another; what remains a point of contention, however, is our vision of objects placed one behind the other.

1196. And yet, in that man is not thought of as stationary, but as capable of movement, this is the most reliable theory because of the parallax.

1197. Strictly speaking, the theory of the use of corresponding angles is here included.

1198. Kant deliberately confines himself within a certain sphere and is always ironically pointing beyond it.

1199. For a long time people have been busy with the critique of reason; I could wish for a critique of human understanding. It would be a true benefit for humanity if common sense could be convincingly shown how far it can reach, that is, precisely as far as is needed for life here on earth, and that's all.

1200. 'Strictly speaking all philosophy is only human understanding in "amphiguric" guise.'

1201. Human intelligence, assigned in a very special way to the practical sphere, only goes wrong when it ventures on the solution of higher problems; higher theory, however, can rarely adjust to the sphere where the other operates and has its being.

1202. Dialectic is the development of the spirit of contradiction which is given to man so that he can learn to recognize how things differ.

1203. Active scepticism: it is incessantly occupied in overcoming itself so as to attain limited reliability of a kind by means of controlled experience.

1204. The general factor common to this tendency is: to discover whether some particular predicate is really conducive to some particular object, this investigation being undertaken with the idea of being able to apply the tested findings confidently in practice.

1205. A lively, gifted spirit, keeping as closely as possible with a practical intention to what is nearest of all, is the most excellent thing on earth.

1206. The greater our progress in experience, the closer we get to the unfathomable; and the more we are able to profit by experience, the more we realize that the unfathomable is of no practical use.

1207. A thinking man's greatest happiness is to have fathomed what can be fathomed and to revere in silence what cannot be fathomed.

1208. We live in the midst of derived phenomena and have no idea how we are to arrive at the original question.

1209. Everything is simpler than one can imagine, at the same time more involved than can be comprehended.

1210. We must note the curious fact that people are not content with what is simple to understand, but go straight for the more complex problems which they will perhaps never grasp. What is simple to grasp is quite usable and useful, and can keep us occupied for a whole lifetime if it satisfies and stimulates us.

1211. We should inquire into the phenomenon, treat it as accurately as possible and see how far we can get with it by insight and practical application, while allowing the problem itself to remain at rest. The physicists act in the opposite way: they go straight for the problem and, as they go, they get involved in so many difficulties that in the end every prospect disappears.

1212. That is why the Petersburg Academy has received no answer to its prize question; and extending the time limit will not serve the purpose either. The Academy should now double the prize and promise it to the one who very clearly and distinctly demonstrates why no reply has been submitted and why there could be none. Anyone capable of this would have richly deserved any and every prize.

1213. Even now the leading scholars in the natural sciences declare the necessity of research in the shape of monographs, that is, of an interest in details. This, however, is not thinkable without a method which reveals an interest in the whole; once this has been attained, there is certainly no further need to grope around in a million details.

1214. Only he who finds empiricism irksome is driven to method.

1215. Descartes rewrote his *De Methodo* several times, and in its present form it still cannot be of any help to us. Everyone who perseveres for a while in honest research has to alter his method some time or other.

1216. The nineteenth century has every reason to pay attention to this.

1217. Completely empty words such as those of the decomposition and the polarization of light must be banished from physics if anything is to come of it. But it is possible, indeed, it is probable, that these ghosts will go on haunting the scene right into the second half of the century.

1218. One shouldn't take offence at this. Precisely that which no one admits, no one wants to hear, has to be repeated all the more often.

1219. He who wants to defend what is false has every reason to tread softly and profess refined living. Whoever feels that right is on his side must tread boldly; being right in a courteous manner doesn't make sense.

1220. Laying hold of the truth demands a much higher approach than what is called for in defence of the truth.

1221. All hypotheses hinder the process of 'Αναθεωρισμός, of reconsidering, of contemplating objects and questionable phenomena from every angle.

1222. Hypotheses are scaffoldings erected in front of a building and then dismantled when the building is finished. They are indispensable for the workman; but you mustn't mistake the scaffolding for the building.

1223. When you liberate the human spirit from a hypothesis which has been a needless constraint, has forced a man to see falsely or in part, to make false deductions instead of looking, to brood and ponder instead of judging, to indulge in sophistries, you have already rendered him great service. He views phenomena more freely in other circumstances and combinations, he arranges them in his own way, and the chance of making his own mistakes is restored to him, a chance which is invaluable if, as a result, he himself soon understands his error.

1224. The phenomenon is not detached from the observer, but intertwined and involved with him.

1225. The metaphysics of phenomena proceed from the greatest and the minutest things made present to the human mind only by artificial means; what is particular and is accessible to our senses lies in the middle and on this I depend, for which reason I bless from my heart the gifted people who bring these regions within my reach.

1226. Who can claim that he has a bent for pure experience? Everyone thought he was doing what Bacon had urgently recommended, and who succeeded?

1227. He who has a phenomenon before his eyes is often already thinking beyond it; whoever only hears talk of it, thinks nothing at all.

1228. Phenomena are without value except in so far as they allow us a deeper insight into nature or if they can be applied to our use.

1229. The only significant thing is the constancy of phenomena; our own thinking about them is quite immaterial.

1230. No phenomenon is explicable in and by itself; only many of them surveyed together, methodically arranged, can in the end amount to something which might be valid for a theory.

1231. Theory and $\frac{\text{experience}}{\text{phenomenon}}$ are opposed to one another in perpetual conflict. All union in reflection is deceptive; it is only by action that union can be achieved.

1232. In order to make something theoretical popular you have to describe it as absurd. You yourself must first of all introduce it as practical; then it's valid for the world at large.

1233. It is quite correct to say: the phenomenon is a result without a cause, an effect without a reason. It is difficult for people to find a cause and a reason because they are so simple that they are hidden from view.

1234. A thinking man errs more especially when he inquires into cause and effect: both of these together make up the indivisible phenomenon. He who can understand this is on the right road to action, to doing.

1235. Genetic procedure shows us better approaches even if it is not, in itself, sufficient.

1236. The most innate, most necessary concept, that of cause and effect, leads to countless, constantly repeated errors when it is applied.

1237. A great mistake which we make is that we always think of cause as being close to effect, as the bowstring is to the arrow which it speeds on its way; and yet we cannot avoid this mistake because cause and effect are always thought of together and are thus proximate in our thinking.

1238. The nearest intelligible causes are prehensile, and for this very reason the most comprehensible; that is why we like to think of ourselves as mechanical, which is higher.

1239. In that we expect the imagination to reproduce and to express the process of creation instead of what is already created, and reason to reproduce and express the cause instead of the effect, we have, in fact, done practically nothing, as this is only a transference of $\frac{\text{perception}}{\text{imagining}}$

but is enough for the person who perhaps in his relationship ^{towards}⁄_{against} the outer world is not capable of achieving anything further.

1240. There is now a really bad habit of being abstruse in the sciences; one gets away from ordinary sense without opening up a higher meaning, one transcends, fantasizes, dreads live perception, and when at last one wants and needs to enter the practical sphere, one suddenly becomes atomistic and mechanical.

1241. Granite much likes to weather in round and egg-shaped form; there is therefore no need whatever to think of the blocks in such forms and often found in North Germany as having been uncovered and rounded by being pushed and rolled about in water.

1242. Fall and thrust: to want to explain by this analogy the movement of bodies in space is really a hidden anthropomorphism; this is the way the traveller covers the ground. The raised foot sinks down, the one behind is thrust forward and falls, and this goes on and on from departure to arrival.

1243. How would it be if, in the same way, one were to make a comparison with skating, where the forward movement is the responsibility of the back foot in that it then takes on the task of giving a further stimulus of this kind, causing the foot at the back again to move forward.

1244. Pointing the effect back to its cause is only a historical procedure; for example, the effect that a man is killed is pointed back to the cause of the fired musket.

1245. I have never used induction for quiet research on my own as I realized its danger soon enough.

1246. On the other hand, I find it intolerable if someone else wants to use it against me, wants to wear down my resistance by a kind of agitated chase and trap me in a tight corner.

1247. I reckon that communication by analogies is as useful as it is pleasing: the analogous case doesn't want to force itself on another, or prove anything; it positions itself on the other side without making a connection. A number of analogous cases do not unite to form serried ranks; they are like good company, which always stimulates rather than gives.

1248. To err means to find oneself in a condition as though what is true just didn't exist; to reveal the error to oneself and others means to invent backwards.

1249. The circles of what is true are in immediate touch with one another; but in the intermundane spaces, error has plenty of room to wander round and to hold sway.

1250. Nature is not concerned about any error; nature itself cannot do other than eternally do what is right, unconcerned what the result might be.

1251. With its boundless productivity, nature fills every space. Just let us consider our earth alone: everything that we describe as bad, unhappy stems from the fact that nature cannot give room to all that comes into being, and far less can it provide it with duration.

1252. Everything that comes into being looks for space and duration; that is why it forces another thing out of the way and shortens its chance of duration.

1253. What is alive has the gift to fit in with the most diverse conditions of outer influences and yet not to surrender a certain definite independence once this has been attained.

1254. Let us be mindful of the fact that all beings are easily stimulated, that the slightest change of condition, every breath, immediately manifests in the bodies a polarity which is really in a dormant state in all of them.

1255. Tension is the apparently indifferent condition of an energetic being in total readiness to manifest, differentiate and polarize itself.

1256. Birds are quite a late product of nature.

1257. Nature has no legitimate capacity for anything which it does not at some point or other accomplish and bring to the light of day.

1258. Not only loose matter, but matter that is crude and compacted, has an urge towards form: whole masses are basically crystalline by nature; in a mass that is undifferentiated and formless, stoicheiometric approach and interrelationship give rise to a porphyr-like phenomenon which pervades all formations.

1259. The most beautiful metamorphosis within the inorganic realm occurs when the amorphous changes into what has form. Every mass has the tendency and the right to this; micaslate is transformed into garnets and often forms mountain masses where the mica is almost entirely eliminated and only to be found as a slight trace-element and a unifying factor between these crystals.

1260. Merchant dealers in minerals complain that amateur interest in their wares is on the decline in Germany and they blame well-informed crystallography for this. This may be true; but, quite soon, the urge to recognize form more accurately will, in turn, reanimate commerce and this will in fact make certain items more valuable.

1261. Crystallography, like stoicheiometry, also perfects the oryctognost; but my own view is that methods of instruction have been at fault for some time now. Instruction manuals intended both for lectures and personal use, and even as parts of a scientific encyclopaedia, are not to be condoned; the publisher can commission them, the scholar not want them.

1262. Textbooks should be attractive; they can only attract if they present the brightest and most accessible aspects of knowledge and of science.

1263. All specialist scholars are at a great disadvantage in that they are not allowed to ignore what is useless.

1264. 'We are more willing to admit our moral errors, faults and weaknesses than our scholarly ones.'

1265. This is because conscience is humble and takes pleasure in being shamed; reason, however, is arrogant, and a forced recantation brings on despair.

1266. This is the reason why truths that have become apparent are at first only admitted without publicity, then circulated quite gradually, so that what has been obstinately denied may, in the end, appear as something quite natural.

1267. Unknowledgeable people come up with questions which knowledgeable people answered as long as a thousand years ago.

1268. As knowledge grows more extensive, an element of disorder is necessary from time to time; it usually happens as a result of newer maxims, but always remains provisional.

1269. Professional people remain in close contact; the amateur, on the other hand, finds it more difficult when he feels he has to follow suit.

1270. This is why we welcome books which inform us about new findings discovered empirically as well as about newly favoured methods.

1271. This is very necessary indeed in mineralogy where crystallography makes such great demands and where chemistry undertakes to determine detail more closely and to order the structure as a whole. Two who are welcome: Leonhard and Cleaveland.

1272. When we find something known to us explained via a different method, or possibly even in a foreign language, it takes on a curious charm of novelty and a fresh look.

1273. When two masters of the same art differ from one another in their way of expounding it, the insoluble problem probably lies in the centre between the two of them.

1274. Monsieur d'Aubuisson de Voisin's geognosy, which I now have in the translation by Wiemann, helps me in many ways at this particular moment, even though, in the main, it also depresses me; for geognosy, which really ought to be based on a live view of the world's surface, is here deprived of all that is visual and not even translated into concepts, but reduced to nomenclature; in this latter respect it is, admittedly, helpful and of use to everyone, and also to me.

1275. It is not easy to comprehend what is huge and more than colossal in nature; for we haven't got actual minifying glasses as we have magnifying lenses with which to see what is infinitely small. And so one still has to have eyes like Carus and Nees if the mind is to profit.

But as nature is always like itself in matters both the greatest and the smallest, and every dim glass pane transmits beautiful blue colour as also the whole atmosphere with its world-enveloping clouds, I find it advisable to be attentive about sample specimens and to assemble them in front of me. Here what is huge is not now reduced in size, but it is there in miniature and just as incomprehensible as in the infinite dimension.

1276. When, in the sphere of mathematics, the human spirit becomes aware of its independence and feels inclined to follow on into the infinite without further ado, it at the same time inspires the world of experience with such confidence that this world does not fail to make occasional demands. In their turn, astronomy, mechanics, ship-building, construction building of fortresses, artillery, fountain-play, water systems, construction of building blocks, telescope improvers, all these in their turn have summoned mathematics to their aid.

1277. Mathematicians are a strange tribe; because of the great things they have achieved, they have donned the mantle of a universal guild and don't want to recognize the validity of anything except that which fits into their own ambience, and what their organ can deal with. One of the first mathematicians once remarked when a chapter of physics was urgently brought to his notice: 'But is there nothing at all that can be reduced to calculus?'

1278. Wrong notion: that a phenomenon can be dismissed and put aside by means of calculus or by words.

1279. Mathematicians are like a certain type of Frenchman: when you talk to them they translate it into their own language, and then it soon turns into something completely different.

1280. It does not by any means follow that the huntsman who shoots the deer must necessarily also be the cook who prepares it. It may happen that a cook joins the hunt and is a good marksman; but he would be wide of the mark if he declared that in order to shoot well one must be a cook. This is how I see the mathematicians who maintain that it is impossible either to see or to discover anything without being a mathematician, while they really could be satisfied when one brings into their kitchen matter which they can lard with formulas and dress according to their fancy.

1281. We must recognize and acknowledge what mathematics is, to what end it can substantially serve research in the natural sciences, where, on the other hand, it does not belong, and into what a deplorable state of error both science and art have fallen by false application since the time of the regeneration of mathematics.

1282. The great task would be to banish mathematical philosophical theories from those areas of physics where they only hinder insight instead of furthering it, and where mathematical treatment has found such a wrong-headed application by the one-sidedness of the development of recent scientific education.

1283. It could perhaps be shown which is the true way of researching into nature: how this way is based on the simplest procedure of observation, how observation is to be raised to experiment and how, in the end, this leads to a result.

1284. Tycho de Brahe, a great mathematician, was only able to detach himself half-heartedly from the old system, which was at least in accordance with the senses, but which, in a spirit of wanting to be right, he sought to replace by a complicated clockwork, which was neither visible to the senses nor accessible to thought.

1285. As a mathematician, Newton's reputation is so great that his clumsiest error, namely that light, clear, pure, eternally untroubled light should be composed of dark lights, has maintained itself to the present day; and is it not mathematicians who still defend this absurdity and repeat it just like the commonest listener, in words which fail to make sense?

1286. The mathematician is dependent on what is quantitative, on everything that can be determined by number and measurement, and so, in a certain sense, on the universe in its outwardly recognizable form. If, however, we contemplate this, in so far as we are endowed with this capacity, with all our intellect and all our powers, we realize that quantity and quality must be looked upon as the two poles of visible being; which is also why the mathematician raises the language of his formulas high enough, in so far as this is possible, to include the immeasurable world together with the measurable and calculable world. And now everything appears tangible, within reach and mechanical, and he comes to be suspected of secret atheism, in that he, as it seems, believes he can also grasp what is most incomprehensible of all, what we call God, and therefore seems to be relinquishing the idea of God's special or pre-eminent being.

1287. It is true that human capacity to understand and reason is basic to language, but its use does not really presuppose clear understanding, developed reason and an upright will in the one using language. It is a tool that can be used to a purpose and arbitrarily; one can use it just as much for subtly confusing dialectics as for confused-shady mysticism;

one can conveniently misuse it for hollow and empty prosaic or poetical phrases; indeed, people attempt to make up verses which cannot be faulted as verbal prosodic structures, but are all the same nonsensical.

Our friend, the nobleman Ciccolini, says: 'I could wish that all mathematicians would adopt the genius and clarity of a Lagrange in their writings,' that is to say: if only all of them possessed the thorough and clear sense of a man like Lagrange, and would work with such knowledge and such scholarship!

1288. The Newtonian experiment on which the traditional science of colours is based is a matter of the most manifold complication; it includes the following conditions:

> so that the ghost may appear, you need:
> 1. a glass prism;
> 2. this to be three-sided,
> 3. small;
> 4. a window shutter;
> 5. an opening therein;
> 6. this very small;
> 7. a sun image, which shines in;
> 8. shines in at a certain distance, in a
> 9. certain direction on to the prism;
> 10. reflects on a pane of glass;
> 11. which is placed at a certain distance behind the prism.

If you remove numbers 3, 6 and 11 of these conditions, if you make the opening large, if you take a large prism, if you place the pane close by, then the preferred spectrum cannot and will not make its appearance.

1289. There is mysterious talk of an important experiment by means of which this science will be really and truly confirmed; I know it very well and can also operate it: the whole bag of tricks amounts to this, that a few more conditions are added to the above whereby the hocus pocus becomes even more involved.

1290. Fraunhofer's experiment where transverse lines appear in the spectrum is of the same kind, as also the experiments by which a new attribute of light is said to be discovered. They are doubly, or even three times, more complicated; if they were to serve any purpose, they would have to be separated into their elements, which is not difficult for the scholar, but which no lay person has either the necessary knowledge or patience to grasp and comprehend, and for which no opponent has either the will or the candour; on the whole people prefer to accept what they can see, from which they can draw the same old conclusion.

1291. I'm perfectly aware that these words have been written in vain; but may they be preserved as an open secret for future times. Maybe one of these days a man like Lagrange will take an interest in this matter.

1292. As for some time now my *Theory of Colours* has been in great demand, it has been necessary to provide newly coloured plates. As I work at this little job, I have to smile about the inordinate trouble I took to make palpably clear both what is reasonable and what is absurd. By and by, both will be grasped and recognized.

1293. Newton's error is so neatly set out in the encyclopaedia that all one has to do is to learn this octavo page by heart so as to be rid of colour for the rest of one's life.

1294. The battle against Newton is really being carried on in a very low region. One is contesting a badly envisaged, badly developed, badly applied, badly theorized phenomenon. He is being accused of a lack of caution in his early experiments, of intentionality in those that followed, of precipitation in his theorizing, of obstinacy in his defence, and overall of a half-unconscious, half-conscious lack of straightforwardness.

1295. A hundred grey horses don't make up one single white horse.

1296. Those who combine coloured lights to make up the single, basically clear entity of light are the real obscurantists.

1297. Anyone who gets used to an erroneous concept of this kind will welcome every kind of error.

1298. That is why we quite rightly say: 'Whoever wants to deceive people must first of all make absurdity plausible.'

1299. Light and spirit, the one in the physical, the other in the moral realm, are the highest imaginable indivisible energies.

1300. I don't object even if one thinks one can feel colour: this would only serve to activate its own characteristic nature.

1301. It can also be tasted. Blue will taste alkaline, yellow-red sour. All manifestations of characteristic being are related.

1302. And doesn't colour really and truly belong to the face, to sight?

Sketchy, Doubtful, Incomplete Jottings

1303.   Religion: old people.
            Poetry: religion of young people.

1304.   Nature is always Jehova.
            What it is, what it was, and what it will be.

1305. That Christ perished in Hamlet-like fashion, and, worse, because he called men around him whom he dropped, while Hamlet perished only as an individual . . .

1306.   Anthropomorphism,
            Erotomorphism.
            That it dissolves and transforms into moral-sensual feeling
               everything that happens.

1307. Pure nature mentality is an alien condition. The purer the mentality, the less need for the condition. The more complex, more interesting the condition is in itself, the more it lays down the law for our mentality.

1308. Unlimited intellect which appeals to every intellect, which is immune to the attack of common sense, even if feeling does not always determine it.

1309.
                    Constancy
                    (as) with (and yet)
                    antithesis.

1310. It is not true that life is a dream; it only seems so to one who takes his repose in a stupid way, hurts people in the clumsiest way.

1311. Epicurus, who was a poor old man like myself, has been badly misunderstood in stressing painlessness as the most important thing.

1312. It is a special pleasure to talk, and talk at length, about things to people one loves, and to rouse emotions, even if one knows that what one is saying is not true.

1313. People are surprised that I know things better than they do, and no wonder, as they often consider wrong what I think.

1314. We mustn't be afraid to give way when we are contradicted.

1315. People who put their knowledge in the place of insight. (Young people.)

1316. What is false (error) is usually more comfortable for feeble people.

1317. If people knew where what they are looking for is situated, they wouldn't be looking for it at all.

1318. Goodness of heart takes up far more room than the roomy field of justice.

1319. The more unselfish a man is, the more he is . . . subordinated to those who are selfish.

1320. Whatever you do for them is not enough, what you did for them is as nothing; their whole career that you have made possible they look on as an act of God's favour, and so one is as though one were not and never had been.

1321. In worldly matters the only things to be considered are ways and means and tradition.

1322. Rapid strides towards the aim without a thought for the means . . .

1323. As if, in order to procure some timely advantage for the son who lies in the cradle, one were to kill the father.

1324. Thoughtlessness by which we fail to recognize the value of the present moment.

1325. The kind of character which, when portrayed, yields no picture, when pragmatized no result.

1326. Three things are not recognized except in the due course of time:
> a hero in wartime,
> a wise man in a rage,
> a friend in need.

1327. Three classes of fools:
> men because of pride,
> girls by love,
> women by jealousy.

1328. The following are mad:

he who tries to teach simpletons,
contradicts the wise,
is moved by empty speeches,
believes whores,
entrusts secrets to the garrulous.

1329. Who has to practise forbearance?
One who proposes to do great deeds,
is climbing uphill,
is feeding fish.

1330. Jewish attitudes:
Energy as basic to everything else.
Immediate purposes.
Not one, not even the least, the most insignificant Jew who does not reveal marked aspiration, in fact hither-worldly, temporal, momentary aspiration.
Jewish language has an element of pathos.

1331. A German was already absurd even while he was filled with hope; and once he was defeated, he was quite impossible to live with.

1332. Suggestion for the practice of polemical purism in schools.

1333. Aid by subject-matter which poetry has been giving itself in recent times by the use of significant themes, by religion, and the world of knight-errants.

1334. Instances of how people come to terms with the unexpected, indeed, the intolerable, by means of poetical forms:
absolute power appearing empirically,
Oberon, Bluebeard.

1335. Difficulty of achieving within oneself identity of raving enthusiasm and merciless criticism.

1336. The influence of authors, who are well-known by name and are thorough workers. Counter-influence of those who are anonymous and work in the journalistic mode.

1337. A witty humorist as a kind of poet, who, mindful of his great knowledge and emotional power, feels impelled to express himself in metaphors.

1338. Passages of dim writing where the author's intention does not come across clearly to us, and which, because we love him, we first of all analyse, about which, when we return to them, we always feel a certain uneasiness.

1339. I find it marvellous to see tragic guilt, guilt so tragic that there is no need for a tragedy to follow it.

1340. Rendering the spirit dull by sophisticated wit.

1341. English plays.

> Infamous in subject-matter,
> Absurd in form,
> Reprehensible actions,
> Confounded English theatre!

1342. Hersilie said about the mad pilgrim: 'When I want to lose my reason, a fancy which sometimes takes me, this would be the way.'

1343. The sublime, for us who are ultra-sublime, most worthy of veneration, and who yet, looked at closely, are tied to an absurd, indeed infamous, empiric nature – the sublime pulls us up short and makes decision difficult.

1344. There is an unknown quality of lawfulness in the object which corresponds to the unknown quality of lawfulness in the subject.

1345. Beauty presupposes a law that is made manifest.

Example of the rose.

In flowering blossom the vegetative law reaches its highest manifestation, and the rose would then again be the summit of this manifestation.

Seed-vessels can still be beautiful.

Fruit can never be beautiful; because there the vegetative
law recedes into itself, into mere law.

1346. Law which is made manifest, in the greatest liberty, according to its very own conditions, gives rise to objective beauty, which must, of course, find worthy subjects to apprehend it.

1347. The impossibility of rendering an account of beauty in nature and in art; because
1. we would have to be familiar with the laws, according to which nature in general intends to act, and does act, when it can, and
2. be familiar with the laws according to which general nature, in its particular form of human nature, wants to act productively, and does so act when it can.

1348. The beauty of youth can be understood from the above. Old age: gradual recession from manifestation. How far can what is in the process of ageing be called beautiful. Eternal youth of the Greek Gods.

1349. Everyone's persistence in character, right up to the summit of human existence, without any thought of return.

1350. Beauty: every mild, high harmony of all that makes an immediate appeal without any need to ponder and reflect.

1351. Perfect artists are more indebted to teaching than to nature.

1352. The highest intention of art is to show human forms as sensuously significant and as beautiful as is possible.

1353. Frederick the Second on horseback in painted tin on the model of Chodowiecki's statue can be bought in Nuremberg; as a rule he leads children's tin soldiers and even there he is venerable.

But for my part I wouldn't like to see him with my own eyes in this guise in life size, and even less in colossal size.

1354. You really ought to make drawings of your patriotic subjects! A king who is seated in meditation on the conduit of a fountain! Well, if only you could draw his thoughts!

A king of this kind has [nothing] to do with your plastic art; he should only be honoured in spirit and in truth.

1355. Draw, engrave on copper, pay, sell, reward – always keep quite silent – and when you are reproached, let it be; but don't incite anyone to laugh to scorn ever more loudly in the world's hearing these miserably bad products!

1356. If you say: 'This is how we do it,' then no one objects; but if you say: 'You ought to do it like this too, limit yourself according to our limitations,' you're too late by far.

1357. Paris is open and Italy will be open too; as long as our breath lasts, we will point the artist towards the wide expanse of the world and of art and towards the confines of his own limitation.

1358. Don't limit the artist by such [. . .]; in any case, everyone feels limited enough even in his widest enjoyment of the world and of art.

1359. To take pleasure in one's limitation is a miserable state to be in; to feel one's limitation in the presence of the best is indeed frightening, but this kind of fear elevates us.

1360. When we look at works of art, both poetic and pictorial, of the third and fourth century, we can notice how long artists went on clinging to the good old spirit when this had already died off all around them. This is a way of explaining these works of art. They cannot be called abstruse, but can be seen as plastic. See, e.g., the Capitoline bas-relief with Prometheus.

1361. What is humane, lovable, tender in an imaginary form of art: the friar hermit, Sternbald.

1362. Organic nature: alive even in what is minute; art: felt in what is smallest.

1363.   Conflicts

        Leaps of nature and art,

        Genius appearing on the scene at the right time.

        Not crude and rigid.

        And not as yet used up.

        Similarly with organization.

Here, too, nature only leaps in so far as all is already prepared to an eminent degree as something higher appearing in reality.

1364. That 'nature', which is our concern, really isn't nature any longer, but is a quite different being from that which occupied the Greeks.

1365. The Greeks designated as 'entelechy' something potential becoming actual, a being that is always in active function.

1366. The Greeks, when they described or recounted, spoke neither of cause nor of result, but told of the outward appearance.

    And in the natural sciences, they made no experiments, as we do, but confined themselves to single experiential cases.

1367. Function is existence thought of as action.

1368. All effectiveness is more powerful at the central point than towards the periphery. The space between Mars and Jupiter.

1369. Original phenomena: ideal, real, symbolical, identical. Empiricism: their unlimited multiplication, therefore hope of help, despair about completeness.

Original phenomenon

      ideal as the last thing recognizable,
      real as recognized,
      symbolical because it understands all cases,
      identical with all cases.

1370. Economy of experience.
   The Deluge of experience.
   Things one would not talk about if one knew what is being
    discussed.

1371. How the unconditional can condition itself and can in this way put the conditional on a par with itself.

1372. That the conditional is at the same time unconditional. Which is incomprehensible even though we experience this every day.

1373. Empiricism heightened/expanded to the unconditional is, of course, 'Nature philosophy'. Schelling.

1374. That man is seldom capable of recognizing law in an individual case. And yet, if he recognizes it in thousands of cases, he will surely have to find it again in the individual case. The spirit saves itself great detours.

1375. To make for orderly arrangement, and system, in nature research, both hinders and furthers.

1376. All that is in the subject is in the object and also something
    more.
   All that is in the object is the subject and also something more.
   We are doubly lost or secure:
   If we allow the object its greater extent,
   If we rely on our subject.

1377. Every [phenomenon] is accessible like a *planum inclinatum* that is easy to climb if the rear portion of the plane stands there steep and out of reach.

1378. Perspective laws: which with great meaningfulness and also correctness refer the world to man's eye and his point of view, and in this way make it possible for every strangely confused crowd of objects to be transformed into a clear, calm picture.

1379. All relationships of things among themselves – true. Error exclusively in man. Nothing true about him except that he errs, cannot find his relationship to himself, to others, to things.

1380. Knowing: what is significant in experience, and what always points towards generality.

1381. The history of scholarship: what is likely to interest people in every age?
How have people gradually tried to give an account of this or to pacify inquiry?
The history of knowledge: what has gradually become known to man? How has he behaved about this and with regard to it?

1382. Scurrilousness of the early Middle Ages right up to the sixteenth century, making first-rate people like Aristotle, Hippocrates ridiculous and hated by spreading silly tales.

1383. The man who has dealings with corporations is always unhappy. Von Humboldt is not allowed to report anything except what is valid in Paris. So what is to become of everything we call knowledge and science? It will all look quite different in a hundred years' time.

1384. Well-known sayings which are repeated as an isolated, if not fortuitous yet unrelated saying, but were discovered by a genius in the context of a sequence and because of that sequence.

1385. Not only barbarians with fire and sword, not just clerical obscurantism: the scholars themselves are barbaric obscurantists who . . . [MS breaks off].

1386. In matters of controversy, note who has hit on the salient point.

1387. Mathematics always concerned with . . . [MS breaks off] and a worthy object. Compared with willing and poeticizing.

1388. Mathematics which is out for conviction, for a convincing proof, which is why it irritates clever people.

1389. One hears that only mathematics is certain; it is no more certain than any other form of knowledge and activity. It is certain when it confines itself wisely only to things about which certainty can be attained, and in so far as certainty is attainable.

1390. That is precisely the outstanding thing about mathematics, that its method immediately shows where there is a stumbling block. Is it not a fact that they found the path of celestial bodies not in accord with their calculations, and therefore turned to the conjecture of disturbances, these disturbances still being too many or too few?

1391. In this sense one can designate mathematics as the highest and most certain science. But it cannot make true anything except what is true.

1392. And how does the mathematician relate to conscience, which is surely the highest and most dignified heritage of man, an incommensurable activity which is operative in the most delicate way, dividing and then reuniting itself? And it is conscience from the highest to the lowest. It is conscience in one who writes the smallest poem well and outstandingly well.

1393. If these hopes are realized, so that people unite with all their powers, with heart and mind, with reason and love, and get to know one another, then things will happen which are as yet beyond anyone's imagination. Mathematicians will condescend to be received into this general moral world-league as citizens of an important state and will gradually shed the conceit of lording it as universal monarchs over all else; they will no longer presume to declare negligible, inexact, inadequate everything that cannot be made subject to computation.

1394. All crystallizations are a realized kaleidoscope.

1395. Even among those who took a friendly view of my way of seeing things, no one has ... [MS breaks off].

1396. It was already common in Roman times that when people wanted to say something really clever they said it in Greek. Why don't we say it in French?

How is it that a foreign language is more [helpful] to express a rare emotion ... [MS breaks off].

1397. The question about the instincts of animals can only be resolved by the concept of monads and entelechies.

Every monad is an entelechy which appears, given certain conditions. A thorough study of organisms lets [us] into the secrets ... [MS breaks off].

1398. Unpretentiousness should be an integral part of good, close-structured society. In a larger social group pretentiousness is always and from the start at an advantage, but forthrightness, indeed coarseness, belongs to a popular gathering where the lower classes want to have their say, people whom one has to shout down, or else one has to hold one's peace and slink off home. However, I can ... the Newtonian rabble, whether made up of 'folk', of pharisees or of learned scholars who ... [MS breaks off].

1399. What is true, recognized, as well as what is false, presumed, all are [put] side by side ... [MS breaks off].

1400. The incurable evil of these religious quarrels is that one side wants to derive what is of the highest interest to man from fairy tales and empty words, while the other side wants to find the cause in a context where no one can calm down.

1401. I of course expect that many a reader will contradict me; but surely he will have to accept what is there in black and white in front of him. Another, with the same copy of the book in his hand, will perhaps agree with me.

1402. Because if one pushes aside problems that can only be explained dynamically, then the mechanical kind of explanation again becomes the order of the day.

1403. How greatly we have been occupied with granite! It has been associated with newer epochs, and yet none comes into being before our eyes. If this were going on in the lowest depths of the ocean, we would have no knowledge of it.

1404. It is best, therefore, if, when making observations about these things, we remain as conscious as possible of objects and of ourselves when we reflect on them.

. Addenda from the Posthumous Papers

1405. Man can only live together with his own kind and not with them either; for in the long run he cannot bear the thought that anyone is like him.

1406. The most mediocre novel is still better than mediocre readers, indeed the worst novel still participates in some way in the excellence of the genre as a whole.

1407. Actors win hearts and don't give away their own; they cheat, but do it with charm.

1408. The Germans know how to correct, but not how to give supportive help.

1409. Whichever way you look at nature, it is the source of what is infinite.

1410. You have to have actually found a thing if you want to know where it is situated.

1411. He who acts as though he's glad, and is glad about what he has done, is happy.

1412. Impatience is punished ten times over by impatience; one wants to draw the goal closer and is only moving it further off.

1413. Young people are nature's new *aperçus*.

Notes

These notes are mainly restricted to brief publication details of the various parts of the collection and to information which is helpful for an appreciation of individual maxims. Generally, however, where an allusion is irrelevant to our understanding, no note has been supplied; likewise, details of sources have been provided only in cases where they are deemed useful. Cross-reference has also been restricted.

When a subheading, followed by a page number, is given, the note refers to the subheading itself. Otherwise, the note numbers correspond to the maxim numbers as they are given in the main text.

Ottilie's Diary (p. 3) Ottilie, one of the central characters in *Elective Affinities*, records both events and maxims in her diary. The narrator of the novel suggests that most of the following are less likely to have come from her own mind than from a book from which she has copied out those that struck her.

Art and Antiquity (p. 8) Goethe began publishing the periodical *Über Kunst und Alterthum in den Rhein- und Mayn-Gegenden* (*Art and Antiquity in Areas of the Rhine and the Main*) in 1816; it provided a steady outlet for his maxims until it ceased publication in 1828.

94 Armand du Plessis, Cardinal de Richelieu (1585–1642) had instigated the attack by the Académie Française on Corneille's *Le Cid* (1636), an action which led to the author's adopting a more conventional approach in his succeeding plays.

96 *Inferno*, Canto 25, where Dante (1265–1321) describes the revolting transformation of a human being into a reptile. The idea of progressive change and development for better or for worse, of 'metamorphosis' in Ovid's sense, had a life-long fascination for Goethe.

123 Tycho Brahe (1546–1601), the Danish astronomer, and Seneca (c. 3 BC–AD c. 65), the Roman writer and philosopher, who maintained that comets were not merely passing, but recurrent phenomena.

157 Goethe devoted considerable energy to disputing Newton's theory on the nature of white light, and a number of maxims are directed against him and the spectrograph. Newton's famous treatise appeared in 1704 and was translated into Latin in 1706. Goethe conducted his fierce campaign against what he saw as the falseness of Newton's theory from 1790 until his final years. Maxims 156–9 are all concerned with Newton (1642–1727), as also, in particular, is no. 431.

Own and Assimilated Material (p. 19) As the subtitle to this section makes clear, Goethe did not seek to conceal the fact that some of his ideas were drawn from others. In a number of maxims later in the collection, Goethe acknowledges quotation from others by using inverted commas.

182 This Whitsun hymn, 'Come, O Creator Spirit', has been frequently translated into German and other languages; Goethe saw it as a prayer to the artist's creative inspiration and himself translated it, entitling the poem *'Appel an's Genie'* (letter to Zelter, 12–14 April 1820).

205 'Phanerogamy' is a botanical term concerned with the sexuality and fructification of plants; a 'cryptogam' is a flowerless plant.

211 Goethe is probably referring to converts of his own time, in Italy and at home, who often were, in the terms of the next statement, 'problematic' characters.

221 Archimedes (*c.* 287–212 BC), the Greek physicist, is credited with the dictum 'Give me but one firm spot to stand, and I shall move the earth'; Karl Wilhelm Nose (1753–1835), a Danish geologist and contemporary of Goethe, countered the latter with his own version, 'Take where you stand'. The implications of the final statement (G. = Goethe) are unclear. The author could be seen to be suggesting the importance of justifying, and standing firm on, one's own position. See also no. 549.

228 The quotation is from *Historiae romanae* by the Roman historian Gaius Velleius Paterculus (*c.* 19 BC – after AD 31). Goethe has in mind Mantegna's *Triumph of Caesar* (1484) where the Roman general is shown as triumphalist as possible. (Mantegna's nine canvases were bought by Charles I in 1627 and are now in Hampton Court.)

231 The song quoted here is that by the Harper in *Wilhelm Meister's Apprenticeship Years*, Book II, Chapter 14. The queen was Luise of Prussia, tragically banished and living in exile at Memel. It was Luise's sister, the Duchess of Cumberland, who told Goethe about the powerful impact of this novel and of its healing solace.

232 Cf. note on no. 96. Domenico Zampieri (1581–1640) would be of particular interest to Goethe, the amateur artist, as the former's landscapes form a connecting link to those of Poussin (1594–1665) and Claude (1600–1682), Goethe's greatly admired models.

235 Hiddensee is an island in the Baltic. Goethe may have taken this curious expression from Dähnert's dictionary of Low German, *Plattdeutsches Wörterbuch* (1781).

243 Timon of Athens was a notorious misanthropist, but the idea seems to be Goethe's own, and he expressed it elsewhere.

251 Johann Georg Hamann (1730–1788), a particularly cryptic mystical thinker beloved of the Pietists.

253 The outspoken journal of the Silesian courtier Hans von Schweinichen (1552–1616) was not published until 1820–23, when Goethe read it with relish.

258 Marie-Jeanne Roland was guillotined in Paris on 8 November 1795.

259 'Polypragmosyne': incessant activity.

260 In 1824 Thomas Carlyle (1795–1881) sent Goethe the German translation of Captain Thomas Medwin's *Journal of the Conversations of Lord Byron* (1824).

269 The influence of Friedrich von Raumer, whose monumental history of the Hohenstaufen dynasty was published in 1823–5, is clear from Goethe's comments in nos 267–71. Ludwig Wachler was a literary historian.

273 In 1824 the psychologist Ernst Stiedenroth published an inquiry into the nature of the soul. In his review of this book Goethe stressed the author's interesting use of Aristotle's term 'entelechy', suggesting each individual's innate capacity to grow and develop.

279 In 1829 Goethe published the correspondence between Friedrich Schiller (1759–1805) and himself. The friendship linking the two poets was admirably analysed by Thomas Carlyle in his *Life of Friedrich Schiller* (1825).

305 Taken from a letter by Madame de Sévigné, but an idea already expressed by Goethe in no. 22.

311 An ironical comment about the German vogue for philosophical idealism.

322 There has been some difficulty over the interpretation of this maxim. Goethe was an admirer of the mathematical clarity of Spinoza (1632–77), while he shared the general unease over Machiavelli (1469–1527), author of *The*

Prince, a tract which advocated ruthless power politics. The maxim would seem to suggest that an excessively mathematical approach to poetry is comparable to being ruthless and immoral in one's reflection.

339 The oracles of Trophonius deprived inquirers of the capacity ever again to laugh.

340 '*Gemüt*' suggests emotional disposition and feelings.

355 The 'Aristotelian' Unities of time, place and action, firmly adhered to in French classical models, were forcefully rejected by Goethe in his first major play, *Götz von Berlichingen*. He nevertheless seems to be suggesting that a three-act play, in which the Unities are observed in each act, can be artistically successful.

358 A play wrongly attributed to Shakespeare.

Brocard (p. 46) This subtitle was supplied by one of Goethe's editors, Riemer, who suggested in a letter that the concept was not to be understood in the sense of the 'legal sentences' used by 'Burchard' or 'Brocard', a medieval Bishop of Worms, but rather as combining pithy, witty or sarcastic ideas.

From the Periodical Issues on Morphology (p. 47) Goethe wrote extensively on morphology, that is, the study of the form of animals and plants, and he collected much of this material in six separate volumes which appeared over the period 1817–24. Maxims 391–418 were first published in *Zur Morphologie, Zweiter Band* (1822).

391 'Monad': a concept known to Goethe through Leibniz's *Monadologie* (1720), and used here (as in the following reflection) in the sense of an indivisible unit. Leibniz (1646–1716) had argued that the whole world is composed of 'monads' which are grouped into complex structures to make up everything that is both animate and inanimate.

404 In *German Poetics* Goethe condenses a much longer title, *Grundzüge zu einer theoretisch-praktischen Poetik, aus Goethes Werken entwickelt* (1821) (*Basic Outlines of a Theoretical-Practical Poetics Developed out of Goethe's Works*), by Joseph Stanislaus Zauper (1784–1850), while the 'appendix' which Goethe mentions was a later volume, *Studien zu Goethe* (1822).

419 Collected writings on various aspects of science, *Zur Naturwissenschaft überhaupt* was a sequel to *Zur Morphologie*. Maxims 419–40 appeared in 1823. Despite the rather disparaging title ('almost out of date'), Goethe's satisfaction with the following section may be gauged by the fact that it also appeared in a newspaper (controlled by his publisher) in the same year.

431 A further example of Goethe's intolerant attitude towards Newton and all who supported him (such as Malus), and approval of those who opposed him (such as Seebeck and, in the next maxim, Reade).

432 In Joseph Reade's *Experimental Outlines for a New Theory of Light, Colours and Vision* (1816), Goethe found support for his long-standing arguments against Newton's theories concerning the colour spectrum.

436 The English Oxford and London Society eventually became The Royal Society, established in 1662. In *Geschichte der Farbenlehre* (1810), Goethe outlines the history of the gradual formation of scientific societies in England and France, not as yet possible in uncentralized 'Germany'.

From Wilhelm Meister's Journeyman Years (p. 57). For details of the strange manner in which the following maxims came to be featured in *Wilhelm Meister's Journeyman Years*, see the Introduction.

468 Immanuel Kant (1724–1804) made a clear distinction between pure reason, knowledge as such, and practical reason, knowledge acquired by experience, by the senses, the particular domain of the artist. In Goethe's view, German art was too often dominated by ideology.

542 Gotthold Ephraim Lessing (1729–81), playwright, critic, philosopher. Goethe misquotes slightly from the original, betraying his loose manner of working in certain maxims.

599 'Geognosy': a knowledge of the structure of the earth, in particular the mineral character, grouping, and distribution of particular rocks. 'Geology': a more general concept, the science of the earth's crust, its strata, their relations and changes. For Goethe's use of the word 'reason' (*'Vernunft'*) here, see no. 555, where it is contrasted with 'understanding' (*'Verstand'*). 'Geognosy', and its relation to 'dead' or 'living' phenomena, is also referred to in no. 1274.

609 Joseph-Louis Lagrange (1736–1813), famous mathematician and long-serving President of the Academy of Sciences in Berlin.

633 Numbers 633–41 are translated from the Latin text of Plotinus' *Enneads*, V, Book 8, which Goethe found to his taste; the continuous text of the original is given the form of separate maxims.

657 'A self-torturer': the concept comes from a comedy by Terence (?195–159 BC), based on one by the Greek comedian Menander (342/1–291/90 BC).

705 'Stereometry' is a branch of geometry which deals with solid figures. The maxim is suggesting that in its beginnings nature could be reduced to geometrical formulae.

713 A famous compliment to the greatest writer of aphorisms in German, Georg Christoph Lichtenberg (1742–99), scientist and writer. His *Aphorisms* have appeared in translation in Penguin Classics (1990). See also Introduction.

717 Sisyphus was tormented in Hades by being eternally forced to roll a large rock up a hill, from the top of which it always rolled down again. Vulcan was cast out of Olympus, falling to earth and breaking his leg in the fall.

The inverted commas used for this maxim indicate a quotation, but the source has never been identified. It has commonly been assumed to be Schnabel's *Die Insel Felsenburg*, mentioned in the following maxim. See also note below.

718 Albert Julius is the central figure in an early 'Robinsonade', a story in the style of *Robinson Crusoe*: J. G. Schnabel's *Die Insel Felsenburg* (originally published in 1731 and newly edited in 1827 by the Romantic Ludwig Tieck) was always of great interest to Goethe.

731 Christoph Martin Wieland (1733–1813), a versatile and highly popular writer; Goethe would have in mind his playfully erotic rococo verse.

742 'Yorick' was used as a pseudonym by Laurence Sterne (1713–68); he is also a character in Sterne's *Tristram Shandy* (see following note).

743 The maxims 743–59 and 773–85 are translated from a text by Richard Griffith. Goethe, with whom Laurence Sterne's novel *Tristram Shandy* (1759–67) was a great favourite, thought that Sterne himself was the author. Since Goethe has translated rather freely at points, a translation of Goethe's own German is here provided rather than Griffith's original English (available in the *Deutscher Klassiker Verlag* edition by Harald Fricke, pp. 888–93).

No. 786 is taken from a letter from Sterne to D. Garrick, while 790 is taken from Griffith, who is in turn quoting Terence. Nos 795 and 796 are also from Griffith while no. 797 is from the Roman philosopher Marcus Aurelius, as quoted by Griffith. Some critics have speculated that other maxims in this section may also derive from the same source.

766 Frederick the Great of Prussia despised German poets and dramatists in comparison with the French, and in his tract *De la littérature allemande* (1780), he expressed his scornful disapproval.

773 William Warburton (1698–1779), bishop of Gloucester, was a conventional traditionalist theologian, to whom Sterne's attitude would have been anathema.

786, 790, 795, 796 and 797 See note 743, above.

808 'Brontotheology to Niphotheology': Goethe avoids the expected suffix '-ology' to create neologisms: 'the *theo*logy of thunder and of snow'.

812 Johann Kepler (1571–1630), astronomer at the court of the emperor Rudolf II. He discovered and described the laws of the planetary system.

816 '*Luxe de croyance*': 'the luxury of belief'. The phrase is taken from Madame de Staël's *De l'Allemagne*, published in Germany in 1814.

817 '*Praedestinatio*': 'predestination', the doctrine that God has determined the outcome of everything which will come to pass.

868 'Party spirit' not in a political sense, but rather the feelings engendered within the crowd.

969 Cardinal Jules Mazarin (1602–61), an astute French cleric and statesman, successor to Cardinal Richelieu.

984 Apollo Sauroktonos: 'Apollo, the lizard-killer', a classical image which Goethe may have encountered in 1812. The original statue was by Praxiteles (*c.* 370–330 BC), who is praised in no. 1097.

1027 Goethe intensely disliked negative criticism, a point which emerges in several maxims, and he therefore likens his critics to Ate, goddess of evil, who was hurled from Olympus to earth and injured in her fall.

1036 Sakuntala: drama by the Indian Kalidasa, known to Goethe since 1791. See also no. 1041 and note.

1041 Kalidasa: Indian writer of the fifth century AD. Pedro Calderón de la Barca (1600–1681), a prolific dramatist of the Spanish Golden Age who was ordained as a Catholic priest and whose works are frequently religious in spirit. Goethe spoke positively of his works in other contexts.

1043 Friedrich Gottlob Klopstock (1724–1803), famous poet and early influence on Goethe; the maxim represents an uncharacteristically negative assessment of Klopstock's great epic, *Der Messias*, completed in 1773.

1044 'Schmidt von Werneuchen': Friedrich Wilhlem August Schmidt (1764–1838), pastor of Werneuchen, a poet of modest ability.

1045 Eulenspiegel: eponymous hero of an anonymous collection of comic narratives, extremely popular in the sixteenth century, and still read with pleasure in Goethe's day.

1063 'Cantilena': simple or sustained melody, as in plainsong or lullaby.

1064 The first four of these unpublished maxims on art were directed against Johann Gottfried Schadow (1764–1850), sculptor at the Prussian court, of whose naturalist and nationalist tendencies Goethe disapproved.

1079 'Systole', 'diastole': medical terms applied to the contraction and dilatation of the heart, but often used by Goethe in a broader, metaphorical sense. 'Syncrisis' and 'diacrisis', as the maxim suggests, represent a comparable activity.

1088 Albrecht Dürer (1471–1528), German painter and engraver, famous especially for his woodcuts. The rather negative view expressed in this and the following maxim is balanced by far more positive assessments elsewhere in Goethe's writing.

1090 Martin Schongauer (1445–91), famous for his engravings of religious scenes.

1093 Klopstock (see 1043 above) was the first German poet to break free successfully from rhymed verse; Johann Heinrich Voss (1751–1826) provided German translations into verse of the *Odyssey* and the *Iliad*; Hans Sachs (1494–1576) was famous for his lines in rhyming pairs, which seemed primitive by comparison with late eighteenth-century models. There is some irony in this remark, since Goethe himself had admired and imitated Sachs's method at an early stage of his career.

1097 Praxiteles, Greek sculptor, one of whose motifs is referred to in no. 984.

1098 Jan van Huysum (1682–1749), Dutch master of still life, greatly admired by Goethe.

1131 Daniel Nikolaus Chodowiecki (1726–1801), Polish painter and illustrator who became Director of the Berlin Academy. Goethe particularly appreciated his scenes of ordinary life.

1182 'Aguillonius': François d'Aguillon (1566–1617), Belgian physicist to whose work Goethe refers in his studies on colour.

1191 Anaxagoras (*c.* 500–428 BC), Greek philosopher, mathematician and astronomer, whose fragments Goethe studied on several occasions.

1200 'Amphiguric': 'dark', 'confused'. The inverted commas suggest a quotation but the source has not been identified yet.

1212 In 1827 the Petersburg Academy offered a substantial prize to anyone who could explain the nature of light. Goethe wrote a whole essay in criticism of their offer.

1215 René Descartes (1596–1650), French mathematician and philosopher whose *Discours de la méthode* is referred to by Goethe in his major study on colour. In his autobiographical *Poetry and Truth* Goethe distances himself from Descartes's overly rational approach.

1258 'Stoicheiometry': the process of calculating weights and volumes in a chemical reaction.

1261 'Stoicheiometry': see 1258 above; 'oryctognost': an expert on minerals.

1271 Karl Caesar von Leonhard (1779–1862) and Parker C. Cleaveland (1780–1858), geologists and mineralogists; Goethe held the work of both in high regard.

1274 'Geognosy': see no. 599 and note.

1275 Karl Gustav Carus (1789–1869) and Christian Daniel Gottfried Nees von Esenbeck (1775–1858): fellow scientists and friends of Goethe, capable of grasping the great as well as the small.

1287 Ludovico Ciccolini (1767–1854), Professor of Astronomy in Bologna; for Lagrange see no. 609 and note.

1290 Joseph von Fraunhofer (1787–1826), who in 1810 discovered dark lines in the spectrum of the sun.

1342 'Hersilie', 'the mad pilgrim': characters in *Wilhelm Meister's Journeyman Years*.

1361 'The friar hermit': an allusion to a work by the Romantic Wilhelm Heinrich Wackenroder, *Herzensergießungen eines kunstliebenden Klosterbruders* (1797). 'Sternbald' is the central character in Ludwig Tieck's Romantic novel *Franz Sternbalds Wanderungen* (1798).

1373 Friedrich Wilhelm Josef von Schelling (1775–1854), exponent of Nature philosophy and indebted to Goethe for his early intellectual development.

1383 Alexander von Humboldt (1769–1859), famous scientist and friend of Goethe's, was a member of the French Academy of Sciences.

Addenda from the Posthumous Papers (p. 178) It might appear that the maxims in this final section are questionable in some way, coming as they do immediately after those that are sketchy or incomplete. This is not the case, however. Hecker simply seems to have placed here the small number of maxims which he did not see fit to incorporate in the main four sections of posthumous items that are given above.